ALL SCIENTISTS
DIE SICK

ALL SCIENTISTS DIE SICK

VINCE P. HENNESSY

Charleston, SC
www.PalmettoPublishing.com

All Scientists Die Sick
Copyright © 2021 by Vince P. Hennessy

First Edition

Paperback ISBN: 978-1-63837-518-0

"It is possible that a scientific discovery will be made that humans will later regret because it has awful consequences. The problem is, we probably would not know in advance and, once the discovery is made, it cannot be undiscovered."

-Paul Davies

"It sounds cliched, but superheroes can be lonely, vain, arrogant, and proud. Often they overcome these human fatalities for the greater good."

-Tom Hiddleston

TABLE OF CONTENTS

ACKNOWLEDGMENTS

This book and storyline ended up being a project far larger than I could have ever imagined, and the journey took over four years to complete. I started it when I was fifteen and didn't finish it until I was halfway to nineteen. Along the way, I met many new people and connected with some friends in ways I never had before. Their faith in me and their hope is part of what helped me combat myself, as my procrastination, laziness, and habit of being easily distracted, which were the main reasons that this project took so long to finish, were invisible forces that I could not battle alone. I have already written hundreds of pages for this, so it is only right that I take the time to write a little more and thank everyone who has helped me finish this story.

I'd like to start the acknowledgments off by thanking the man who was the biggest initial help when it came to creating this book, and that's my **Chief Scientific Editor, Mr. Michael Kelly**. While the title may be fictional and a joke between him and I, it holds true to his part in helping me. Not only is he an excellent teacher, but he is a passionate man when it comes to science, and he spent a lot of his time discussing a lot of the theoretical science that is in this series. In fact, his class is where I got a lot of my ideas from, and you'll notice that a lot of the science revolves around biology. Halfway through senior year, he and I ended up never talking again, but he still means a lot to me because he had a significant impact on my life both in school and out of it. So, I thank him, because the truth is that he didn't have to help me confirm the theoretical possibilities of scientific manipulation on a scale that most high schoolers don't even think about. Also, out of everyone, he seemed to have the most faith and pride in me when it came to finishing the book, and he couldn't believe I was working on such a project, so I thank him.

Continuing with teachers and their influences, I honestly have to thank **Ms. Deborah Quinlan**. She was my English teacher before high school, and before the idea of this book ever existed, but my ability to write was actually discovered in her class. While she had no intention of digging it up, a writing prompt she had given us, which was focused on creating a strong opening paragraph for a story, actually led to me writing a draft for a book. While that story, which only ever got to seventy-two pages, was put aside, I began writing ever since that class, so I have to thank her. It just goes to show how talent can spawn anywhere at any time, and that sometimes, the assignments teachers give us can affect our lives in more significant ways than we think.

While these two teachers were not a major part of this book's creation, **Mr. Giorgi Tchubarbria** and **Mrs. Laura Fucilli** were a part of strengthening my will to finish this book and publish it as well as two of my favorite teachers. They are extremely kind and passionate teachers, and they encouraged my science and writing skills.

Moving on from teachers, I have three best friends I'd like to thank because, unlike everyone else, they were stuck hearing about my book on a daily basis. Of course, they got in their own jabs and insults, but they were all supportive, they helped with some ideas, and they always made sure to ask how progress on the book was going. I'll start with **Steven Agalopoulos**, as he had to hear about my book more than anyone. I cannot express enough gratitude for **Owen Ingrey**, who has not only endured hearing about my book almost daily, but he has also been a great influence in my life in many ways, and a true best friend for years now.

Then, the last of my friends, I'd like to thank **Matthew Carroll II**, who is, unfortunately, my enemy now, as he and I had several conflicts, but before that, he was a major part of my life. While he made fun of my book more than anyone, he was actually really interested in it. More so, he liked that I wanted to be an author, as he had secretly been creating a lore of his own for several years, and he spent every day at lunch for almost a year telling me about it. If it were ever a book, it would be a series with each book thousands of pages long, and I couldn't believe how much time, effort, and creativity had been put into the fictional universe. His lore makes my book seem like a prologue at most. While he didn't help me with my book, Matthew changed my perspective on life. I realized that there are *so* many amazing stories and fictional universes out there that, just like his, aren't being written or published because of fear of failure or lack of faith in one's self. That drove me to write and publish my book because I realized that it could be the story that could have changed someone's life but never did because of doubt. It's what drives me to help others bring their stories to life because some of the stories that we personally and we as a society need to hear are not there since some people are afraid to write, and I don't want it to be that way. Every story deserves a chance. So, despite our parting of ways, I have to thank Matthew for changing my view on writing and showing me that it's so much more than just a story idea I wanted to share.

Then, there are two family members that I'd like to thank. The first is my **Godfather Joey**, as he always supported me and offered to help me in any way I needed. Without a doubt, I also have to thank my youngest sister, **Isabella**, who was the most major help when it came to this project. While she isn't a co-author, her level of assistance almost reaches that point. From listening to every idea and possibility to proof-reading and suggesting, she was actively involved in supporting, creating, and editing the fictional universe I had made. I can't thank her enough for everything she does both regarding the book and my life. Without her, I would not be here today as a person or an author.

I promised my close friend, a secretary of my previous workplace, that I would mention him in the acknowledgments. He didn't help at all with my book,, but he is an excellent friend. Out of all the people I've met, he's been the most intriguing person to enter my life so far, and my deep conversations with him have changed my perspective on a lot of things, and he reinforced my beliefs in a lot of things. In a way, he has been a bit of a mentor to me, and he has taught me much about people in the real world, and I shall apply those qualities to characters in future stories. So, as much joking around about putting him in the acknowledgments as I have done, I would actually like to really thank **Ian Smith**, who better be happy to see his name in the bold font here. Along those lines, I'd also like to mention and thank **Giovani Trook**.

Finally, there are the remaining people, who, unfortunately, cannot all be named. As I mentioned earlier, this book series, due to both myself and several other factors, took a long time to write and edit. Instead of being wrapped up in a few months as it should have been, it took more than four years, so I met and talked to many people about it during that time, especially at work. So, I'm unable to remember everyone I need to thank, and I won't go into detail, but I want to thank the following list of people for their support regarding my future, my decision-making skills, my beliefs, and my ability to write and publish such a large book (now a series) while still just a high schooler. They've all meant a lot to me, and I hope that they will continue to.

I have to thank beachgoers **Mr. Rick, the Lerner family, Joe, Ms. Jill and her family, Madelyn, Ms. Irene, her husband,** and most importantly, **Ms. Betsy Flynn, her family, and friends**. Not to forget those I met near the end of my journey writing this series, to include the **Duncan Family, Summers, Swain, Tall Johnson, Ruth K**, and **Mike S.**

A special shoutout and thank you to two very important people in my life, **Gabrielle G.** and **Nathan D.**

I'd also like to thank Sedge Islanders **Maggie, Makena, Destiny, Gabby, AJ, Caroline, Nicole, Victoria,** and **Bryan.**

AUTHOR'S INTRODUCTION

If anything has been rewritten more times than this series, it would be this author's note. Originally, this book series was just a single book that spanned over 1,300 pages long. Now, that initial book has been broken into six individual books, all about 200 pages long. The journey to get to this point has been long and hectic. It's been exhausting, to be honest, and I'm very glad to be at the end of it. My passion for this series was great, but the unexpected obstacles I faced along this path were much greater. I made it, however, and I'd like to share some of the important lessons I have learned, how this journey has made me feel, as well as what this series is.

Before it was broken into six books, the original **All Scientists Die Sick** book was rewritten seven times. With each round of what I thought was going to be final editing, I ended up adding a hundred or more pages because the story just kept growing and growing, along with my skills as a writer. This book has drastically changed over the past four years, with the addition and subtraction of many chapters, scenes, characters, relationships, and plotlines. I started writing this book halfway through my sophomore year of high school, and I finished it just before the end of my senior year, only to end up working on it again for almost half a year more.

The book was originally called **S.S.S.S.** That work-in-progress title was an acronym standing for **Stupid Short Sci-fi Stories,** and the book was just meant to be a collection of short story ideas I had that couldn't make it on their own as an entire book. In fact, it wasn't a serious project at all, and it was primarily just a mental break from the second major book draft I had been working on for a religious-fiction book that I was passionate about. I wanted to continue writing every day, but I needed a break from the religious-fiction draft because it was such a big project. Ironic, as this book ended up being an even larger project that took far longer to finish than I would have liked.

The first story in **S.S.S.S.** was going to be a tale of a man who could teleport but lost either his recent memories or almost all of them. On his left arm was a tattoo detailing where he could find a journal that had everything important about him written down. Another idea was that he had to have his memories travel separately when he teleported and would have to inject them into himself, as shown by his tattoo. Either way, the short draft was leading up to a day where the man could not find the journal or serum, and it resulted in a journey of self-discovery and change. The plot twist at the end was going to be that his butler or caretaker had actually hidden the object on purpose so that the main character, the man, could become a better person.

The second story- cliche as the planned plot of it was- was to be about a person who enjoyed torturing others. As a fun writer's thing to do, I decided I would have an "Easter egg" in it. The main character of the second story would use a weapon from the company owned by the man in the first story. The idea was just to show that the stories were both happening in the same world, but that simple connection was actually the first stone in a long path leading to the final product before you now. What started out as the name of one company from one story appearing on a weapon in a different story quickly became an intertwining system of different people and detailed backstories. The short stories which had all just been a collection of various ideas picked up from biology and history class ended up having one thing in common: the stories were all hard science fiction. What was written within their plots were scientific theories and ideas that are theoretically possible, and some that are even on the verge of happening. In fact, as I spent years working on this project, some of the fictional theories and inventions I had been writing about came true, which was both uncanny and frustrating, as people would believe my stories came after the realities, but it was and is the other way around.

That was only the beginning of the long journey, however, for halfway through writing this book, the idea for a sequel was created, and so the ending of this book was created to match what would come. Then, there was another book that went along with those two, and then another one and possibly two more. Soon, I realized not only that my writer's subconscious was far ahead of me, but that what was supposed to just be a collection of worthless stories ended up being a whole new universe in the realm of literature: one where real-life and fiction are one interchangeable existence through science and technology.

All Scientists Die Sick has been the biggest project that I've ever worked on or even thought of. I've sacrificed a lot of valuable time to write, and I've actually sacrificed a lot more for this book than anyone would ever guess or be able to understand. Even though the ideas were all there, and I'm a fast writer, time management was a major issue. Besides being a procrastinator, lazy, and easily distracted, I was constantly being pulled away from writing my book by school, my family, my career, and life in general. While I believe that this book is like fine wine or cheese- that its process of aging makes it better than what it originally was- the journey to finish this book was a long and exhausting one. It went from being a passionate project to almost being a burden, and no author wants to feel like their book is a burden. After two years, my passion had dwindled, and I was tired of reading the same lines over and over again. There was a horrible part of me that wanted to just forget about the story for a while, and possibly forever. However, I continued on as new scenes, characters, and plots grew and developed, adding on to the complex story. I *needed* to finish and publish this book, not only for me but for everyone I had promised. A lot of people had expressed their belief and hope in me, and I didn't want to let them down. Then, I also knew that I needed to finish this book for that kid one day whose life will change from reading the story, as books can change lives. The endless pains of this writer's journey are ones that I will forever carry alone, but I hope that the entertainment and lessons brought about by this book are ones that we can all enjoy together. Thank you for reading this series, because it means *everything* to me. I truly hope you enjoy it.

At least, that's where I thought my author's introduction would end. After all, I was done writing, and my book was going to be published. Yet, my writing ability is both a blessing and a curse, and after professional formatting, my book came out to be over 1,300 pages long. It was too big, and I was forced to break my book apart into a series. I have many mixed feelings about the series as a result, as I never wanted to write a series. However, it was necessary if I wanted to be an author and have my story shared with the world. While it was not too difficult to split my book into a series, it was another major obstacle I faced along my journey, and at the very end, which made it all the worse. As the final book in what might end up being the first half of a longer series, book six kept the original title of the initial book. I also kept the acknowledgements and author's note in this specific book, as well as the dedication and quotes. That's because this book marks the final part of my first writing journey, even if it is just the beginning of many more to come.

This last paragraph isn't for the readers or for me, but this part of the introduction is for other writers out there. I was depressed and discouraged to hear that my book couldn't be published because it was too large. It hurt me financially and emotionally, and I wanted to quit writing and forget being an author. I wanted to get rid of the 1,300 pages of content and wipe my story from existence. After months of delays and after all I had been through, the last thing I wanted to hear was that my book would be delayed even more. In fact, what was supposed to be a single book published in September ended up being a series that wasn't fully published until late June. Giving up was so much easier, even if it meant all I had sacrificed and bore would have been for nothing. I didn't, however, and pushing through the pain, I ended up with a series that is six books long, and that's absolutely incredible. People won't understand. They'll say I'm dramatic. In fact, no one thinks it's that hard, nor have I even been respected as an author since everyone treats it as a joke. But it's hard. I'll bear it all alone for a *long* time, but at the end of the day, despite it all, I have my own published book series, and I've made myself proud. As long as it's able to change one person's life, I'll be satisfied. So, please, if you're a dreamer, a writer, or want to write, keep writing and keep trying. Writing isn't easy, and publishing is a lot harder, but don't give up. It *will* be worth it. Your story will go far beyond what you ever imagined, so long as you allow it to. Thank you

CHAPTER 1

BATTLE AFTERMATH

(Homestead, Florida. April 18, 2022.)

A failed hero, his body and spirit terribly injured, Timothy looked around in a desperate effort of spotting ***The Sinful Son*** escaping with Sir Thomas, but no one was around. The only people in the area were the incoming police and the S.W.A.T. Units that were accompanying them. Timothy knew that it was time to go, as there was nothing left for him there except for consequences.

His muscles sore and his movements languid, Timothy started walking across the street when he saw Kronos half-limping out from behind one of the smashed police cars. "Woah there! Stop moving, man! You've got a bullet in your leg," Timothy exclaimed as he pointed to a dark stain underneath Kronos' right knee.

"Is that so?" Kronos muttered without care as he rolled up his pants leg and looked down at the injury. "Ah, correct. I didn't even really feel or see it until now, but one of those cops accidentally shot me through the black smoke. It was from far away, and my skin is thick and covers bones that are almost eight times denser than regular bones, so I'm relatively fine. Manmade weapons that are not of the experimental level pose no threat to me, and it's probably by my own power alone that I could be defeated since I stand above all others. Still, I should've made the pants bulletproof besides just the lab coat and the R.N.T. Suit, but it's what it is. There's no need to worry about it."

Timothy looked at the wound. The bullet had not penetrated too deep into the skin. He winced in disgust at how dark Kronos' blood was before the wound was covered back up. "If you say so. Compared to how the rest of us turned out, you're actually quite lucky."

"It *is* quite a mess. This street is chaotic, and many lives were lost today, though mostly insignificant ones as far as I'm concerned. All that matters is us three. Where's Thomas?"

Hesitantly, Timothy hung his head in utter shame. "I'm truly sorry, Kronos, but I failed you, myself, and everyone here, along with the future generations. We thought he was defeated, but The Dark Depressor got him. Sir Thomas bravely saved me. I didn't know-"

Faster than he could react to it, his nervous system readjusting to normality, Timothy was instantly slammed against the smashed police car by Kronos, who tightly gripped the failed hero's neck with the deadly Atomic Gauntlet. "That's damn right, Timothy! You failed miserably, and if we don't find Thomas, I'm going to fucking tear you apart on an atomic level! For all of your heroic talk, you ended up being worthless and useless in that battle. I stayed uninvolved for your sake because I knew how much this battle meant to you, but if I had known that the old geezer was going to be a gentleman up until the very end and trade his life for your pathetic one, I would've destroyed everyone here instead. He means a lot more to me than people would think, and I'm glad your father is dead and can't see what happened here today. You tore apart your own family for your dream, and then you threw that dream out because your obsession with it made you reckless. Was it worth it, Timothy? The future that's coming is one that only I can prevent, but after meeting you, I changed my mind because I realized that maybe some of the rival scientists were strong enough to continue onward, but you've proven me wrong! You've let me down in every way! I was originally correct, as always, and I weakened to the level of a human and changed my mind because your heroism inspired me. Now, I'm-"

"I know!" Timothy yelled out through tears. "But for right now, we have to get out of here, and we have to leave *now*! The cops are here with backup, and we'll be arrested, so let's go."

⚛ ⚛ ⚛

Back at the house, it was eerily quiet, and the two men knew it was only a matter of time before the household grew more chaotic than it had been out on the street. Stella had been preoccupied upstairs when the men arrived home, but she would come downstairs, and once she saw what was going on, there was no doubt that there would be tears and yelling.

In the kitchen, Kronos was sitting in a chair with his injured leg prompted up on a chair across from him, using his high-tech sunglasses and vast intelligence to analyze his wound. Timothy was in the bathroom, shaving away his slight beard and, after debating for a minute, getting rid of his new mustache. As Timothy moped into the kitchen to help out Kronos, Stella walked into the kitchen, screaming at the top of her lungs upon seeing Timothy in his costume, and Kronos' injured leg.

"Silence," Kronos commanded. "It's not as easy for me to assess the severity of my injury with you screeching over there like an untamed banshee. Take your shock out on your son, not me."

"*Timothy*! What the *fuck* is going on here? Your hair is all coarse, and there's grey in it, and *what* are you wearing? Is that a hero's *costume*? *And* what is *that* on my kitchen table?" Stella asked in violent disbelief as she started pointing to the R.N.T. Suit on the kitchen table. "What's going on here? Don't tell me you dressed up to try and stop that voodoo man or something stupid!"

"The only thing stupid here is you! Kronos has a bullet in his leg, but all you want to do is lecture me and complain about me while yelling and cursing. I'm a *real* hero, known as The Chronological Changer, and it's all over the news, but clearly, you haven't been paying attention.

And, we *did* go fight **The Sinful Son**! You think heroism is all some stupid fantasy full of crap, but it's not! I've become the very thing you always tried to stop me from becoming because…"

The arguing went back and forth for quite a while, growing louder and more aggressive with each word as Timothy and Stella verbally battled in the on-going war of ideas that had been started when he was just a young child. Kronos, meanwhile, sat and watched, listening and observing human interaction for himself, finding it all intriguing and displeasing. The drama got extremely personal and verbally violent as the two yelled and cursed back and forth, throwing ideas of heroism and family all over the place. Kronos yawned.

"Shut up, you stupid bitch!" Timothy yelled before uppercutting his mother and then jabbing her in the face with his other hand. "I fucking hate you so much!"

Kronos jumped out of his seat, rushed over, and smashed Timothy in the back with a punch from the Atomic Gauntlet, nearly breaking his spine before he grabbed him from the back of his neck and held him against the fridge. "Now, I've been rather passive and inactive since we've gotten to Florida, and I hate your mother and I'm extremely disappointed in you, but as a man who lost his parents at a very young age, as an honorable and prideful man, and for the sake of all parentless children, intervening on such domestic violence is necessary," Kronos stated neutrally with aggressive honesty. "I cannot allow you to cross the line and inflict physical pain upon a parent when many of us long for one. I understand that you do not consider her your mother and that you truly despise that wicked woman, but you must cool your temper immediately, Timothy. After today's events, it's quite possible that the path of redemption will not be enough for you to ever call yourself a hero. It may be true that only a select few know the truth about what happened today and how much of a failure you were, but a true hero wouldn't be able to live with such knowledge out there. Don't make it any worse or more impossible for yourself."

"You're right, as always, Kronos, but we can't be fighting each other right now!" Timothy coughed out. "Sir Thomas needs us, and he needs us as soon as possible. Whether I end up a hero, a villain, or a depressed bum after this is all over, right now I need to continue being a disgraced hero, just so we can save your caretaker. Got it?"

Kronos let go before taking a step back, and Timothy slid down the fridge, gasping for air. "Of course, I got it. I'm well aware of that, though I'd hate for a disgraced hero to rescue a man whose goal is to be a gentleman. It might ruin his reputation, or perhaps improve it, but I can't be worried about that as of this moment." Kronos looked at Stella, who lay on the kitchen floor, unconscious. "She'll be out for a while, and we should give her medical attention, but that'll have to wait. First, I have to extract this bullet out of my leg. I would have done it on the battlefield, but I got a gulp of that gut-microbiome-attacking gas. Predicting such a possibility, I had already boosted my microbiome to a higher level, but it wasn't enough to fully stabilized me."

"I think we have a first aid kit somewhere, or at least pliers to get that bullet out of-"

"There's no need for you to retrieve any supplies for the operation. After all, my title, though not certified by some pathetic school or test, is *Dr.* Kronos Nephus, and a simple bullet extraction is nothing more than putting cream on a small mosquito bite. Of course, we won't be extracting it in a normal fashion," Kronos said mischievously with a smirk as he pulled out his Deconstructor Blade. Activating the current that coated the outside of the blade, Kronos placed the sharp tip of the knife against the bottom of the bullet before twirling it around in a circle, penetrating deeper into the shell and disintegrating it.

"Wait, stop! Stop!" Timothy shouted as he watched the operation, stepping closer. "You're hurting yourself, Kronos. I mean, you're getting rid of the bullet by tearing it apart atomically, but you're also getting some of your cells along with it. You'll have a hole in your leg."

"Do you know how many times I've been deconstructed and reconstructed? My immune system might have forgotten about my teleportation, and my memories of the pain might be gone, but my cells are separate from my brain's memories, and they're quite used to the feeling," Kronos said through clenched teeth. "Tolerating pain is one of the main things that makes us superior. It's remarkable how the human body adapts." Slowly standing up, Kronos started to put the R.N.T. Suit back on. "I'm heading to the bathroom to patch up this hole and stop the fresh bleeding. While you're waiting, head upstairs to the room I used last night, and we'll create a plan."

Nodding his head, Timothy went upstairs, stepping over his mom, and was soon joined by Kronos. "Glad to see you're perfectly fine, as we're going to need both of us on this mission," Timothy commented as he glanced at Kronos' leg. "I appreciate you letting me have the spotlight, but heroes aren't meant to care solely about fame or recognition, and we're not supposed to be ashamed to ask for help from others, partner. What's our plan? Can you track them somehow?"

"The education system pays its teachers to say that there are no stupid questions, but that could not be further from the truth. What you asked is amongst the endless amount of stupid questions asked every day. Of course, I can track them! I built a tracker into Thomas' suit. I trust him, but I knew that if the rival scientists were to ever take a hostage, it would be the old man without scientific-based powers. You're too fast, and I'm too unpredictable." Kronos opened up his laptop. "The signal seems to have disappeared at a certain point in the ocean, meaning there's a jammer or something. Either way, we're going to rescue that old son of a bitch known as my father, and we're going to end *The Sinful Son's* boss so I can finally continue on with my journey to find a cure."

CHAPTER 2

THE SINLESS SON

(Homestead, Florida. That Same Day: April 18, 2022.)

When Sir Thomas regained consciousness, he was overwhelmed by a sore feeling throughout his body. His eyes, after he forced them open, were able to slowly look around. It was pitch black, and he could not see anything. The only light in the room was on him, and its rays only spread out to three feet in front of him, revealing nothing but a cement floor. His body was strung up, each limb being pulled to a different corner as his body hung there, suspended above the ground. He was a few inches above the floor and an inch away from a wall that stood behind him. Sir Thomas pulled and struggled to move, but the ropes bounding him were tied too tight, and he was too weak.

"An expected reaction of prey is that it will undoubtedly struggle with all it can, both mentally and physically, in an effort to escape what bounds it before the predator that captured it can feast," a monstrous voice stated as glowing red eyes appeared across the black room from Sir Thomas. As the overpowering voice, maliciously whispering like death by undetected cancer, continued to preach, the eyes slowly came forward with each sentence, burning more and more powerfully. *"Then, of course, one must also worry about the dreadful parasites, who will steal you from the predator and make you their*

own meal. Such is the case of the fly within the sinister strands of the spider's web or the death-sentencing cells of a Venus Flytrap's deceitful mouth. What are humans? Prey? Predator? Parasite? Do we have a choice in which one we can be? Does being a predator mean giving up humanity and letting selfishness and survival take over instead of politeness and peace? Is being a parasite wrong or clever? Such questions are rather intriguing, and you'll find that they relate to us more than one could ever imagine. Even I struggle with the questions of the universe and this reality that my unfathomable mind summons during its natural pondering during the blackest hours of the night and the brightest hours of the day, forever turning like a bioreactor blade through conglomerations of negative emotions, powering my existence."

"Bloody Hell! If I wasn't a literary expert after years of reading and studying books, I'm not sure I would've been able to understand a single word of what you just said," Sir Thomas replied. He chose to speak freely, as he was not afraid of death or ***The Sinful Son***, and he was hopeful and almost sure that Kronos and Timothy were on their way to rescue him. He could imagine their grand entrance. "I already had a headache from being knocked out, but you've gone and made it worse. You're quite the talker, and you ask a lot of unanswerable questions. Then again, I'm not surprised that you speak so sophisticatedly. Out on the street, you were rhyming quite a *lot*, but now I see that you are *not*."

There was a sound of metal cracking like human bones snapping and being crushed into fragments. ***"You would dare to, at such a perilous time, choose to speak to me in rhyme? To do so is condemning and has insulted my pride and honor, and you'll undoubtedly end up a goner. However, what you pointed out was not wrong. You speak the truth, as I do not constantly rhyme all the time. It is random, and typically used when I am getting a point across to someone I am preaching to. Of course, my emotions also affect my rhyming skills, which are the greatest in all of existence, both past and future. Connecting words in such a delightful and clever manner comes*** *naturally without pause or a moment to forcibly think of what would match perfectly or slant just right. As far my most notable dialect, which is, undoubtedly, difficult for any mere mortal to interpret and understand, I'm quite grateful that your years of wisdom and literature grant you the honor and privilege of speaking to me on a level that no other could ever hope to achieve."*

"Well, I'm honored, and you're quite welcome."

The fiery red eyes stopped a few feet away from Sir Thomas, and they hovered there in the darkness, seemingly innocent and menacing at the same time. *"After all, that'll make our conversation all the more pleasant, like dining on high-quality lobster and pheasant. Despite my monstrous identity and the fact that you're bound by rope, I urge you to continue on with hope. I'm not a man who tortures or is harsh and cold, especially when it comes to people who are old."*

"I prefer to be called advanced-in-age, rather than old. Sure, I've been alive for quite a long time, but my body is still going strong, and will, hopefully, continue too. If a pleasant conversation is what you seek, then I will happily indulge and humor you for now. It's not like I have anywhere to go, at the moment. I'll stick to what you were just monologuing about a moment ago. Tell me, *The Sinful Son*: have you given up humanity and more to become a predator? Were you once prey, trapped by others?"

The Sinful Son chuckled menacingly. *"Your answers and questions are indeed seeds that you, a clever farmer who has sowed and harvested countless times, are trying to plant within the rocky soil of my mind in the hopes that you might become my master or bribe me with what you have grown. The untilled soil of my mind is rocky and barren after suffering seemingly endless years of drought, and it is no longer able to sustain or bear any kind of plant life, no matter how good the seed might be. Nothing but tumbleweeds and decayed plant life exist there now, and they have deteriorated past the point of being able to recover and grow again, no matter how much water or fertilizer blesses the land. That truth aside, I shall answer your question, for I am not a man of secrecy or insecurity, and my life is one that all should know before they die and go. I am neither a predator nor a being that is prey."*

"Well, I'm gobsmacked," Sir Thomas said sarcastically. "I figured you weren't going to choose one of the two options you gave me. After all, there are always more options than life or people let you know about. Neither a predator nor a being of prey? An interesting response. You *were* quite dodgy and terrifying out there on the street, and I doubt any of us could have stopped you besides Kronos. No offense to Mr. Godwin, of course. Are you still human? Quite honestly, I'm beginning to believe and expect that anything is possible after these past few days."

"Unfortunately, or perhaps, fortunately, I am still human and always shall be. It is a truth of this universe that the feeling and idea of humanity within us all can never truly be destroyed or gone. Only with death itself can we possibly part ways with the humanity in our souls, whether they be clean or dark. I was once more human than anyone else. My heart and head were filled with ideas of a closely-knitted and loving family, goals of being a true gentleman, ideas of mutual love that were purely deep intimacy and respect, and every other traditional and perfectly happy concept society had to offer. The peaceful life I longed for, the future I truly wanted, the plans I tried, and everything else that was great about life and the idea of it... they were all permanently taken from me."

"Oh? I figured that was the case."

"As expected, as the horrors of my past have so deeply scarred me and mutilated me that any person is capable of seeing and knowing that I suffered what no other could hope to endure. I was a being of utter sympathy and empathy, combined with a protective personality that automatically and naturally made me the guardian angel of anyone I encountered, and I cared for everyone deeply upon meeting them if we got along. My humanity went far beyond the emotional

levels of others. So, try as I might or fail to stop it as I might, the monstrosity you fear cannot completely take over my mind and body. The most remarkable thing about human beings is that, as I said before, we'll always have a piece of humanity in us, no matter how far we stray from the natural or normal path of life. Whether it's biological, spiritual, or something else, humans can always realize that they've done wrong and try to change. Most won't be able to change or redeem themselves, but all humans are able to know that somewhere in life, at some time of utter failure or hopelessness, they made a mistake or acted rash. All human beings are able to stop and do the right thing, even if it'll mean their downfall or unbearable punishment. Our intelligence in the realm of emotions and knowledge is what separates us from every other living being, and it includes, if not centers around, the idea of humanity, which is a most glorious and most grotesque combination of endless concepts and qualities that I could not hope to name or describe."

Sir Thomas nodded his head, regretting the action, as his neck was aching in pain. He looked up at the pair of red eyes that were a few feet in front of him, burning but motionless. They were simultaneously packed with emotion and were lifeless. "Hmm. I'm still not entirely sure that I understand your personality, but you honestly don't sound like a wanker. There's no doubt that you've done rotten, horrible things that might be unforgivable, but your philosophies are rather intriguing. They aren't the most brilliant, and you're not an ace on the topic of life, as no one is, but I think you and I would get along quite well. You *did* offer to talk instead of fight, and I can't deny that we attacked first. Unfortunately, I'm tied up, and you're a menace, so I'm afraid we're not the best of friends."

"Indeed. It is as you have stated. Yet, your circumstances are in your favor, as unbelievable as that may seem from your perspective. A weakness of mine, or at least one that I had as a young man and child, is that I tend to overly idolize, praise, and admire people. That was especially the case with people I didn't know too well. That

weakness might have been due to my crippling and condemning loneliness, my lack of friends, the absence of love, and not having a family, but it was a weakness that led to utter disappointment. The fact that you and I are talking now is a result of that weakness. Unfortunately, I never had a father or grandfather, in a way, and so, you are extremely fortunate, because I respect and cling to the idea of you, as you are like the men of a family that I lacked growing up. Therefore, I am staying here and conversing with you. You are a clever man who lacks fear due to hope, it seems, and your wisdom might benefit me. If not for all of those compelling factors, I would leave you here in the darkness alone, waiting for her, The Torturer, to arrive. That anxiety-filled wait of dread would be unpleasant for both of us, and I'd rather be here when she interrogates you, as she knows not of bounds or morals anymore. Her mind is far gone. Worry not, as you are merely the bait of her plan, and I shall not allow harm to befall you by her hand or my own."

"Well, blimey! The Torturer? She sounds worse than you, and she sounds like she would torture me. I suppose I'm fortunate then, and I'm extremely grateful. Thank you, **The Sinful Son**. Still, I'm surprised by how talkative and kind you seem to be. I'll take advantage of your troubled youth and my wisdom to converse with you since you've offered. Your philosophies are intriguing, and a few things you said almost left me gobsmacked. That, and I still have nowhere to go or any way of escaping on my own while tied up like this. So, you believe that no one is truly evil, or that we can at least always try to escape evilness? That we go to the edge of evilness but never beyond it because our humanity stops us?"

"That is both correct and incorrect, the ideas of life constantly juxtaposing each other as they always have and existing paradoxically. There are three types of people in this world: those who are born evil, those who are made evil by others or life, and then, there is the third type, which is the worst. Of course, anyone who is born evil can overcome their natural wickedness, as that is what humans are capable of, and anyone turned evil by others can return to the

light of life, and I don't mean Jesus Christ but goodness in general. Either way, people born or made evil can always end up good. No one is truly evil, and as you said, humanity prevents us from crossing the line of no-return beyond evil, which is unimaginable. There are cases of mentally-ill people forgetting or not being able to access their humanity, but those are special cases. My point is, there has only ever been one person I have ever met who was truly vile and despicable. He was my father biologically, but I do not consider him to be a human. He had no humanity. No emotion. No love. He was a being that had never before existed until his birth, and he was born beyond that border of humanity and evil. My mother still had a bit of humanity in her, but it was unreachable. My older sister's youth spared her from being truly evil, as she still had plenty of time to end up good. We all end up moving toward that border, but we can never cross it, and we can always turn around and head away from it."

"Well, that was a lot to take in. I understand what you're trying to say, though, and I agree, for the most part. Some people do seem to be born evil, and other people suffer and turn to crime or hatred. We all sin at one point in our lives, and we all certainly think something evil at least once during our lifetime. Most of us try to overcome our troubles and do the right thing, but having free-will means that we don't have to, so I understand why some people end up evil. I think you're right about not crossing that line, though. Even if evil people don't repent or sacrifice themselves, along the way, a part of them knows that they were wrong or are doing the wrong thing. Whether or not that makes us human is up for debate, but humans are certainly both evil and good. Unfortunately, some people are born evil, and others are turned toward the darkness because of misfortune or others. We all have a major effect on other people, and that even includes strangers. You said that there were three types of villains, and I agree with that for the most part, knowing that each of those three categories can be broken down into smaller groups. For example, people turned evil by others aren't always true villains, but rather, they're like anti-heroes. Which one are you?"

"I am undoubtedly the third and worst kind, which is both of the other two options. Born a monster inside of a human, my young mind thought of the most vile and despicable things that no child should or could think of even with outside guidance and influence. My demonic deeds first began in kindergarten and continued on from there, plaguing my school years until high school. Even as a toddler, my mother once told me that I had issues. That I was a freak and a monster. She always said that. Throughout high school, she called me an outcast and freak as well. Those were her nicest remarks. Yet, I was more human than anyone, so despite my childish deeds that were unforgivable horrible, I tried to be a good person. As I've said before, my goal was to become a true gentleman, a protector, a lover, a father, and so many other roles that society had to offer. Life was meant to be good. I was meant to be good."

"But then you're circumstances began to turn you toward evil and becoming a monster. It was unbearable. You were already struggling with being good because you were naturally born with wicked thoughts and an instinct to devastate, and combined with the evil that was created by others, it was too much too handle. Especially since you most likely kept everything to yourself, as you had no friends or family. Finally, without warning, for no one knew of your internal struggles, you snapped and never returned."

The Sinful Son chuckled softly, the noise contained inside his acidic stomach. *"You're intelligence and ability to connect everything a person says to create an understanding of their backstory and personality greatly impress me. Although, I have begun my return from the realm beyond humanity. What you stated is, undoubtedly, the most truthful summarization of my atrocious life. Its simplicity appalls me, and it lacks countless details adding up to the endless days of the sixteen years that I suffered under the oppressive torment of others, and then the following decades that resulted from the rapture within my being. My backstory is far longer than a few sentences, and if I ever wrote a biography, no mere mortal would be able* *to read it and live. After finishing such a story, filled with unholy truths that reveal the worst of society, humans, families, and ourselves, a person would limp away from the tall brick of paper, crying and murmuring, only to realize that they cannot live any longer knowing what they know. They would choose to ease their pain by killing themself in the most gruesome way possible. So, be grateful that you are able to withstand just knowing that I was born a monster and overcame my natural evilness, only to be turned into an even more vile creature by others, which combined with my biological beastliness. My name is Damon, and my last name is a memory that was attacked and destroyed in my brain during an experiment that The Torturer performed on me. Yet, I would have cast aside that last name anyway, so it matters not. I am simply Damon, and I am-"* Damon stopped short, realizing that what he had just spoken was almost identical to what Elder Damon had said to him during his demonic dream.

"Are you alright, Mr. Damon?" Sir Thomas looked at the blazing red eyes in an attempt to see what was going on emotionally but could, unsurprisingly, determine no facial expression from the artificial features. "You stopped short there as if suddenly gutted. You were talking fine, and then it just went all to pot."

"Indeed, I did stop short in my preaching there, but I assure you that it's not due to a lack of care. Even a supernatural being, like myself, is caught off guard by uncanny events that might be coincidence or something far greater than just that. The mysterious happenings of this world spook even me, and I refer to the patterns and events that we cannot see. I've lost my track of thoughts, so you continue the conversation now, for a trembling feeling is upon my brow."

"Well, then enough of this fancy talk. I suppose I'll get straight to the question that's been on my mind this whole time, Mr. Damon. I'm sure you would have eventually gotten to it, but between you're style of talking and your obsession with the past and all that happened, I'm not too sure if I have enough time left in my remaining years to last until then. Why are you *The Sinful Son*? I don't understand it at all! Why are you attacking people? Why do you dress up and terrorize places?"

"To say that such questions have not plagued my mind as well would surely end with me in Hell. Lying is a sin, is it not? Nevermind that, just know that your curiosity is common and expected, and even I am unsure of what to answer. I am Damon, and I always have been. After overcoming my natural thoughts and instincts of wickedness and evil, I tried to be good, but society frowned upon that as well. If I couldn't be good or evil, then what was I to be? Such a paradoxical and ironic concept made no sense to me. Perhaps, it was fate that I was meant to end up this way, or perhaps, I truly suffered unfortunate circumstances, one after the other, enduring them all like no other, cursed by my father, siblings, and mother, wondering what happened to my missing brother. I was born a twin, though he was far larger than I was, and I'm almost inhuman in size, but he was sent away to an orphanage, as my family could not support more than four kids, so my siblings and I stayed to live. Yet, it was a choice that I wish had not been made, for my brother was the one who was, unknowingly, saved. Besides my regret and jealousy, my parents always used it against me. They had chosen me, and they had chosen wrong. To sing such hateful words was their favorite song, and they sang it for sixteen years long. There came a point where I could bear it no more, and The Sinful Son emerged, starting the on-going war."

"Bloody… Hell," Sir Thomas said in a whispered gasp of grave tone as he thought for a moment. "Could it be that…?" Sir Thomas shook his head.

"Now you're the one who has stopped short in his sentence, leaving it without a proper ending. Something is on your mind, and searching for the answer has sent you back in time. An idea from the past has connected with the present here, and the answer is one that you might fear. As I spoke, a fact of my past set aflame a bulb of light

within the darkness of your skull, but you're unsure if the connection is one that you truly know."

"Well, you said that you had a brother who was your twin. That's fine and all, but you said that he was born larger than you and then sent to an orphanage?"

"Indeed, it cannot be denied, for I have not lied. My brother, from the tales of the past, that as a child, I heard, caused my birthing mother a great deal of hurt. Cut from her insides, he was born an unnatural giant, but he did not cry, and the room was silent. His almost bald head lacked hair, but his eyes were gentle with care. I was born with a head full of hair that was black, and my eyes did not seem to look back, but rather my fists were clenched and ready to attack. Chosen at random, or perhaps debated, they had to send one of us away, and we had no relatives with which we could stay, and so, they made a hard decision after our birth, the next day. Chosen to stay with the family that never would be, the baby sent away was not me. My brother escaped and probably prospered and thrived while I was tortured and barely survived. Why does this tale that you barely know intrigue you as so?"

Sir Thomas laughed lightly. "I'm gobsmacked by your rhyming skills, Mr. Damon. That was literarily brilliant, and you must be an ace in the field of writing. The reason I'm curious is that there's a man I met that was born extremely large, and he's one of the only people I know to surpass you in height. Even more convincing is the fact that he was an orphan for quite a while when he was young until he was adopted and settled down. At least that's what I've heard. The only thing left would be your last name, which I assume would be the same as his, but you don't know it, so there's no point in pursuing the idea. It's a small world, but I doubt you're related to *him*. That would be more gobsmacking than anything I've experienced on this journey so far. Then again, I wouldn't be surprised at this point."

The glowing red eyes slightly shifted up and down as Damon nodded his head. *"That is correct and a point that all shall one day know before they die, as the realization of the uncanny and unstoppable connections and coincidences in this world is an inevitable fact of reality that we all learn and hear about, as well as experience, whether it be in our favor or be our downfall. Besides the fact that all are affected by that phenomenon, it also seems that we're drawn to each other. Not people, but specifically us, as in the people of this world who have gone slightly beyond humanity in the sense of powers and abilities, though we still keep our emotions and minds."*

"Cheers to that observation, Mr. Damon. It seems like every day some new individual rumored to have strange powers is showing up in my life. I'm knackered and rather not deal with it, but I can't say that I'm not impressed and grateful to meet all of these brilliant minds."

"Such is the case with my own journey through life as The Sinful Son. Not only did I meet The Torturer, but I also met and befriended a man who controls metal. Granted, I have not seen or spoken to him in quite some time, but the fact that I met and battled him shows how small this world is. Yet, I think that it's not just the world's smallness, but rather how large we are in comparison to everyone else. Perhaps, it has nothing to do with us being unique individuals at all, and it's merely the fact that humans will seek other beings and humans out that are similar to them because we admire our own selves so much that individuals like ourselves seem attractive and likable, because, after all, they're just like us, but with the improvements that we long for or the flaws we're thankful not to have."

"My God! It *is* a small world, and we are large. You met the guy who controls metal? So did Kronos, from what he's told me, and he was technically on our list. I can't believe that. You battled him?"

"It was a churning sea of the dark unknown that left the surrounding landscape destroyed. His gadgets and the way he uses them is something for all to admire and fear. The only person capable of withstanding such devastating attacks and unstoppable forces of manipulated science is The Sinful Son. Had his strength not been with me, as it always is, I fear I would have been gravely injured

or killed. He was greatly disadvantaged, however, as I am a being created to kill and fight. My power naturally increases with each passing second, as my endurance has almost no end, and my strength is so compacted and powerful that it takes me a minute to get into the fight. Not only that, but my unforgivable and unerasable memories and nightmares play in my mind like video footage that randomly skips from part to part, creating anger, hate, rage, wrath, feelings of revenge, and other violent negative emotions throughout the fight, making me grow stronger and stronger. When he started manipulating my exosuit, I had no choice but to break free from the unholy garments of The Sinful Son. That was his unavoidable doom that devastated him with a series of unstoppable blows far stronger than what he would have expected. After all, my unholy garments are what restrain my unstoppable power. We stopped fighting and talked for a long time, realizing that there was no need for us to be enemies. He is far younger than I am, and he still has much room to grow."

"Bloody Hell! I can only imagine such a battle, and I almost wish I had been there to witness it. However, I'm a bit lost, Mr. Damon. Perhaps, you simply like to occasionally talk in the third-person, but you speak as if you and *The Sinful Son* are two different people or personalities. Is that the case?"

"The undeniable truth of this world and reality, whether people find it a pleasant one or spit in distaste at it, is that only a rare few humans are actually one person, and even they struggle to stay one person. The rest of us, whether you define the two mindsets by personalities or by sides, are at least two people. Some of us are even three or four minds inside of one body, but the point is that we're all more than one person. A lot of us separate our sides into our mouth and our minds, our true selves residing in the skull, and our socially-acceptable selves dancing out of the mouth. Others separate their two sides and personalities into their conscious and subconscious. A small group of the population separates their two sides by day and

night. Others are different wherever they go, and others are different depending on who they're with. Everything I've stated is undeniably true, and it is a fact that has been around for as long as human beings have been around. No matter the method of separation or the reason, we're all multiple people residing within one person. Do you agree with me?"

"For the sake of brevity, as I'm curious about you, I'll just say that I do. After all, you're not entirely wrong, if not wholly correct. I think that people do behave differently around others and in different situations, and I don't doubt that a lot of us keep our true thoughts quiet since they would be frowned upon or judged."

"Then understand that I was born as The Sinful Son and not as Damon. The monster that was instinctively malicious and vile, whose mind was constantly conjuring wicked thoughts beyond a regular child's imagination, who was around for my youngest years of life… that was The Sinful Son. He was untamable until society tamed me. Like most children in life, despite my awful family and the corrupted private school that I was forced to attend, I learned about morals, rules, consequences, and everything else about our society. Like I said, it is often the case that humans develop a monstrous side to them or another personality, or, at the minimum, a side to them that is negative in comparison to how they usually are. I am the exact opposite. Humanity did not exit my mother's womb. From that dark tunnel, an evil being crawled out like it were cast out of the glory of Heaven. I was born a monster first, and then I developed a human side. That is not how it's meant to go. People can recover from their monstrous sides, but they never start off as one. Somewhere… somehow… a seed of humanity was planted into the foul soil of my soul, and it eventually bloomed like a vine that was meant to cover and conceal all of the darkness of the dry soil. So, burying The Sinful Son and overcoming my evilness, which had plagued me since my unholy conception in biological darkness, I became Damon, who was the boy society expected, and the hopeful

gentleman and caring person that I wanted to be, filled with sympathy, empathy, optimism, a longing for love, and everything else that's great about our world."

"I see, and I admire the young man you were. Burying such a monster that lurked in your mind was surely no easy task, and I respect that you tried your best to be a good person."

"It made me proud to know that I had conquered The Sinful Son, and I truly wanted to be good. For a short time, I was the perfect human, and my dreams and beliefs went far beyond what anyone else could hope to be. Yet, my life was not meant to be that way. I had buried my true self, and so, the unfair universe, for I am no longer religious, rejected the forced suppression by having others try and dig up The Sinful Son, whom I had buried deeply within the darkest corners of my heart and mind. All they had to do was utterly obliterate my heart and spirit to reveal him, and the universe knew that, for that's exactly what happened to me. One day at a time, every second of every day, I suffered under the most vile man, who was not human, along with his wife and daughters and brothers."

"I think that we all have rough patches in our family life. I'm not trying to discredit you're suffering, but I'm just stating a fact. You act and say that your family and life were unbearable and truly horrible, but what exactly happened?"

"As I have stated many times before in my life, an endless piece of paper, a single infinite pen or blood-dipped Albatross feather, and all of eternity, would be too short for me to name all that I have suffered. They attacked all of my senses, they attacked every single emotion, they insulted every aspect of my life. They went after my past, present, and future. They lied, taunted, tormented, manipulated, stole, judged, critiqued, criticized, mocked, offended, hated, attacked, destroyed, downgraded, degraded, devastated, demolished, insulted, condemned, and every other negative thing you can think of, toward me. Man before me, who is advanced in age, you would die before being able to finish listening to my life story and

all of the horrors I have endured. I would die before I could tell you everything that I endured. I have over thousands and thousands of pages of journal entries from every single day of my life detailing what I endured, down to the exact words spoken to me. Everything and anything ever done to me or said to me by anyone is permanently engraved not just in my mind, but online and on paper. The words 'unforgivable' and 'unforgettable' exist for a reason, and that's because some words, actions, people, and events are truly unforgivable and negatively unforgettable. Grudges are a part of my unholy power. I can hold an eternal grudge over the smallest aggravation. Grudges are like scars, yet people just want to cover them up or completely erase them from existence. I even have a list of everything my parents ever insulted or said to me that was awful. I could rant and vent for countless days on my family life alone, so ask no more about those wretched beings," Damon bellowed monstrously, his voice, filled with unimaginable wrath, echoing through the condemning darkness of the room. He seemed even bigger and more prominent in the darkness, and his blood pressure was skyrocketing. His breathing was heavy as his heart pounded, his poetry replaced by Hellish curses. *"Do you understand?"*

Sir Thomas, despite not fearing Damon, flinched at his booming voice and its haunting echoes. "Bollocks. I hadn't expected such an angry response, but I understand now just how much you despise your past, and why it's driven you to where you are now. You might be exaggerating a bit, but there's no doubt that you've suffered what no one should."

Damon sighed like a powerful wind from a tornado, the escaping air reverberating with a deep grumble of hatred within him. *"My past is no exaggeration, and it's undoubtedly true that no one, especially a child or teenager, should have to endure such horror to live. However, I had buried The Sinful Son deeply, and Damon tried to stop my family from digging by pushing him further down and trying to refill the dirt holes they made with writing fiction, poetry, television, video games, and working out. Escaping reality temporarily refilled the suppression that kept The Sinful Son dormant. Unfortunately, it wasn't enough, however, as soon, society, teenagers, and life all joined my family, dare I even call them that, in destroying me for no reason. Those pathetic people, influenced by the wickedness of this world or their own stupidity and evilness, didn't realize that by destroying me, they would inevitably unleash the true me that they did not know existed. We should always be careful of the unknown people lurking within others, and be extra sure not to disturb them from their hibernation, for they are locked away for good reasons. Those fools persisted, though. The Sinful Son would either be unburied, or he would burst forth from his suppression to defend Damon and himself. I knew that, and he knew that."*

"Hmm." Sir Thomas had no comments or questions He was captivated by the horrific stories of the past and the formation of Damon and *The Sinful Son.*

"Times were once calm for a bit. The Sinful Son and Damon are almost like two different entities, but we're not. For a while, The Sinful Son had almost completely vanished from Damon's life, though entirely getting rid of me is impossible since I am the original soul. However, I was barely a thought in his head, which flourished as a result, but it was undoubtedly a costly weight in his heart. That was a heavy obstacle that would decay and take away from the process that his mind made, for it made it unsettled and conflicted. It made it lost. Without me, life felt wrong. After all, I was the original creature and he was the outer mold, so with me gone, he was just a hollow being despite how vibrant and alive he was, nor did it matter how much he thrived and prospered, for I was his source of strength. Without my undying hatred, endless rage, and boiling blood running through him, he was left with nothing but a physically fit body. He was a machine that ran, but the boosters and major engine parts were gone."

"Couldn't you just move on a be happy? Why not be at peace? Sure, you had all those wankers and blokes harassing you, but your personal conflicts and battles seemed to have been settled."

"Switching to positive energy would have been fatal, or, at the very least, it would have required far more time than the world would allow him to have, and finding an equal source was rather difficult. Yet, he and I both knew that going back to me as a source of power would be risky, no matter how brief it would be. In fact, that belief was proven no longer than two months after his existence without me had started. Like stepping on a butterfly back in time, the smallest thing brought me back for just a few minutes during an argument with a worthless humanity-lacking peasant. Don't mistake us for two personalities. We aren't that quite yet, and I don't think we ever will be unless something powerful forces our heart and mind to truly split. Yet, it was almost like a personality switch, and even physically Damon felt it. He felt a heartbeat that was not his and saw a face and eyes that were far worse than how his normally were. He felt muscles tense that never did, and his physical strength seemed to increase. His mind thought differently, yet it was not different. Yet, it wasn't any of that which concerned him. It was when the dopamine kicked in along with the switch. The unfortunate truth that being The Sinful Son made Damon, the false personality I had created to replace myself with, feel great like an adrenaline rush filled with dopamine."

"Well, if you were truly born evil, then it would only be natural that you felt good as **The Sinful Son**, and releasing that negative energy and watching out for yourself."

"Indeed. The more I accidentally let him out, the more frequently I could feel him trying to break the mental bars I had imprisoned him in. The more I craved the physical feelings I got as him. I loved being enraged. Soon enough, I heard his voice, which had been silent for many years. I had no recollection of his existence except for the tales of my extreme youth that others had told me. I had grown to believe that Damon was who I was and always had been. The Sinful Son had been hidden from even me. Then, I began to hear his voice and have thoughts that weren't my own. It's not another personality

in the sense of D.I.D. or anything, but I knew he was there, and he only came out when I was enraged or had to survive. Yet, I never let his voice escape through my mouth. I tried my best to stay Damon, but that was when we began to merge. Relying on him in tough situations wouldn't have been wise."

"A shame. It became too much to bear and endure any longer, and so you cast aside Damon and no longer feared the consequences that would befall you if you broke the rules of society, as you were being driven by an instinct to survive. Your importance outweighed the importance of not breaking the laws or your morals."

Damon laughed heartily before sighing sorrowfully. *"That's what most people would assume and believe: that I became selfish because of my suffering, and I chose to fight my oppressors. The Sinful Son is partially inspired by the tale of Jesus Christ. While I don't believe in such a person, whether Jesus was fictional, real, or truly the son of God, he shares the same story that I do. The resurrection is just a bit different. Of course, The Sinful Son was never named until after my suffering technically ended. Anyway, rather than fight and end my oppressors, as that would have been illegal, or run away and suffer and die, I chose to kill myself. My first two attempts ended in mental defeat, and I couldn't go through with it. On the third journey, however, I didn't turn back. As I mentioned before, I was the perfect human being, and that included being selfless. Rather than let him take over me or escape, I chose to end The Sinful Son, Damon, and all of my suffering, while preventing the horrible future that would have been."*

"Bloody Hell! You can't be serious, Mr. Damon!"

"I'm serious," Damon replied with resolve and a selfless tone that seemed uncharacteristic for such a monstrous man. *"We had a small shore house for a while, and there, I was Damon more than at any other place or time, and so, I knew it had to be then and there. If not, The Sinful Son would have merged with me entirely or taken over. Even if it was just for a few minutes or a day, what he would*

do in that time would forever end the life of Damon, and he would be on the run for the rest of all time. So, walking a little over two miles with the morning sky above me dark, I journeyed to my favorite beach street, which, unlike the others at the time, actually had benches just past the cut through the sand dunes. Sitting down, I bled out from my arms and wrists as the sun rose before me, a great ball of fire and unstoppable power. The world would start the day with one less monster amongst society. I had sacrificed myself, and by doing so, I forgave the sins of all who had been against me."

"Wait, but I thought you said you weren't religious? Why believe that you are just like Jesus Chirst? How are you even alive if you killed yourself?"

"Unfortunately, it's undeniably true that the private school I went to was terribly corrupted with phony priests who were despicable, principles who were fakes and unfair, teachers that were utterly incompetent and biased, and students that were not at all faithful or good. However, that was not why I stopped believing. The school was a stepping stone, but the rest of the path was formed by no answers to my prayers, the countless atrocities I endured, and finally, my death. On the other side of my suicide was nothing but blackness. No Hell, no Heaven, no angels, no God, no Jesus Christ… there was nothing. I was brought back to life and saved by The Torturer. She saved me. After my death and finding out how everyone responded, I realized that being selfless on that grand of a level is pointless and foolish, and it always will be. I had sacrificed myself for no reason, and I allowed the enemy to win."

"Mr. Damon, you-"

There was no interrupting Damon, any longer. The more of his past that he told, the angrier and more engulfed in wrath he became. *"I let my emotions take over because that was when The Sinful Son, at the time, was most dominant. Ironically enough, people always say that you shouldn't make decisions when your emotional, but saying that is selfish because people who say that know that an emotional person will actually care about themself and not be selfless. People want you to stop, relax, think, and then make a decision that will benefit them and not you. That's selfish! So, like Jesus Christ, I resurrected, but I went and killed everyone who had been against me. I did what I should have done instead of killing myself. That is why I am The Sinful Son. After dying to selflessly forgive the sins of others, I came back and got revenge, staining my soul and my flesh with unforgivable sin. After that day, The Sinful Son and Damon bonded in an indescribable way, and ever since then, we have simultaneously existed both separately and merged together in a being that should not exist. Even now, we coexist and conflict, but time is tearing me down internally. I'm becoming more like Damon. After all, all of the things that angered me are long gone, other than the daily inconveniences that plague my life."*

"My God!" Sir Thomas shivered, shaking the ropes as he did. His whole body filled with fear and awe at what he had just heard. "That's a story that is unlike any other that I've read or heard, and I can't believe you're real." He gulped. "I'm not even sure what to say."

"After getting my revenge and going on an unstoppable rampage for months, I slowly began to settle down with The Torturer. I spent the rest of my life devoted to becoming an even more powerful and unstoppable being by perfecting my body. I had always been scrawny, but there was power inside of that weak-appearing body that no one would have expected. Yet, Damon did not want to hurt anyone. I didn't want to hurt anyone, so I always restrained myself or just left the conflict. Even now, I sometimes struggle with fighting at full force right away, but I've come to realize that anyone in my way will be pulverized and destroyed, and they don't deserve mercy. I studied every style of martial arts and fighting, both real and fictional, and in the short amount of time that I've lived, I've become a self-trained master in almost all of them. Even the fictional ones are more than capable of being performed in this world and destroying people. Not only that, but I studied and experimented with all of

the body-enhancing techniques and training regiments. My body is impenetrable. My bare knuckles and fingers can rip, tear, and cut flesh. Punches, kicks, and even blades can't harm my hardened flesh, and I've even hardened my bones a bit. During all of that physical training, The Sinful Son calmed down a lot, but I could never find peace. It is nothing but an idea as fictional as utopia. The harsh reality is that peace is truly unattainable."

"I actually have to agree with you on that one," Sir Thomas said with a sigh. "It seems like I can never get a break, and even under ideal circumstances, there's always something on my mind, even if it's just false worries from my mind overthinking. Peace is almost an opinion, though, and so perhaps that's why it's unattainable because opinions are personal and fluctuate. That's the same reason why my allies and I believe that a perfect society, as a utopia suggests, could never exist. We just discussed this recently, actually. Our uniqueness is what prevents that from being made, but people would argue that not being unique and having a utopia of identical people wouldn't be a utopia at all. However, I've rambled on long enough. Continue on, Mr. Damon."

"At first, The Sinful Son was nothing more than an unmotivated genius and a man who was no longer bounded by society, as the people that created society were not equal, fair, or knew of justice and enforcing it. That's why I don't hate that speedster for trying to be a hero. We need those. In a way, though the contemplations of my mind leave me without answers, I am sort of a Byronic hero, and I'm sure that a literary expert such as yourself knows what I mean by that. For a long time, I struggled and grew as The Sinful Son and I converged and repelled each other. Then, one day, I realized that we could be something more than just human. We could be a monster just as society, my family, and the universe wanted us to be. I tried everything to stop it, but I ended up as The Sinful Son. It was inevitable, and perhaps, it was always meant to be whether religious figures or just the universe was doing its own thing. Damon is still here. I haven't crossed to the other side of the border of good

and evil, and I never shall. The life Damon dreamed of and longs for still lights the darkness of my life. I have emotions, morals, I long for love, I understand that I can't have a normal life, and I even have four vows that set me above others. I understand that I cannot be forgiven. There is no normal life for me, and there never shall be. My only escape is death, but I will not die until I help others achieve the same dreams I had. I'm still Damon, and The Sinful Son, who was once The Sinless Son, is also Damon. We are one and two, and we are actually quite unsure of what to do."

"As despicable as you are, I have to agree with that. So, I guess you were right about everyone having a microscopic piece of humanity in them, no matter what. After all, you *are* being relatively kind, and you have been since the start, I suppose. Your past and the justification for your actions aren't entirely excusable, but I can understand why you exist as you do. Before I say anything else in the hopes of saving you, I have to ask: what four vows are you talking about?"

"As The Sinful Son and I combined and repelled each other, I made four vows to myself. Normally, they would have been to God, but I do not believe in such a figure after all that I have been through. I swore them to myself because I wanted to reign above all others, display self-control that would intimidate and scare others, and lastly, my body is a temple of salvation for the broken ones, so the vows made perfect sense. Even my diet of pure life shows how much self-control I have, despite my undying rage. One: I shall not mastur-bate by my own hand, nor shall I ever watch anything pornographic, nor tolerate others who commit sexual assault or rape. Two: I shall never drink alcohol or anything containing alcohol- not even a sin-gle drop. Three: I shall not vape, smoke, consume edibles, or do drugs of any sort. Four: I shall not curse, swear, or use vulgar language, except for the recitation of literature or similar circumstances. These four vows have been kept since I was seventeen. Decades have gone by without me breaking any of them. I am unstoppable. The cursing one is also to restrain my power and ability to verbally decimate

any living being or inanimate object. I alone can create curses and poetry unlike any other condemning kind, and to be able to swear at my thousands of enemies would be too much of an unfair advantage on my part. Also, I'm afraid nothing other than vulgar and foul language would escape my accursed mouth should I be allowed to curse, for my uncontrollable hatred creates an impulsive tongue."

"Well, I'll be damned! I'm actually impressed, and you have my utmost respect and admiration for making and keeping those vows. Any regular bloke probably would've broken one of those by now, especially having lived such a terrible life, so cheers to you. Still, you haven't entirely answered my original question. Between then and now, you've said *quite* a lot. I understand that you were forced to become **The Sinful Son**, at least from your view, but why stay him? If he and Damon exist together and separately, why not live a normal life? You say that's impossible, and I understand that you're racked with guilt and regrets, but if you forgot about everything, you could move on. After all, your oppressors are all gone, aren't they? You said everything that pisses you off is long gone. You disposed of them decades ago."

"There are two reasons why I cannot leave The Sinful Son behind and why he will always be a part of me. The first is that I want to use him and his unholy power, his unstoppable negative emotions of extreme violence and hate, to help others who were in my situation. My life has been condemned to present and eternal suffering, so I might as well spend the rest of it trying to prevent more people like me from emerging. I'm not saying that The Sinful Son and other people like him shouldn't exist, but it'd be better if they didn't or didn't have to, because then, life would be happier and more peaceful for everyone. We have police, and perhaps heroes, to solve crimes and stop the negative actions and events of the real world. There are peace organizations and charities helping provide people with food, shelters, clothing, and everything else they need. There are phone numbers to call for suicidal people. Yet, a lot of kids suffer mental and emotional abuse at intolerable levels every hour of every day

with no one to help them. One day, I'm sure the world will be peaceful, and that such issues can be resolved peacefully. That's the almost impossible goal I'm creating a path toward."

"So, then you *do* believe that peace is attainable."

"It's almost impossible if not utterly impossible, but hope overlooks what is possible or not possible, and I do have hope. For right now, however, I'll use violence, hard choices, technology, and The Sinful Son's unholy power to stop the emotional and mental crimes plaguing households and the lives of countless people. That's all I can do as of right now, and I'll do it because I'm more human and selfless than anyone. My life was ended when The Sinful Son first emerged. If I'm going down, then I'm taking as many oppressors and abusers as I can with me. I am a representative of the broken ones and a savior far different than the kind people expect or hope for. That is why Damon must exist in the shadows and never live his true life. He has sacrificed that for everyone else. The Sinful Son may have first emerged to get revenge and expel emotional energy that would destroy a black hole, but his journey has drastically changed since then. I only wish it hadn't taken me so long to realize that because I don't have much time left, and my body isn't as powerful as it once was. The pure humanity that Damon was made to share is slowly taking over my mind, heart, and soul once again, and he will use the instinctive death-causing thoughts of The Sinful Son in a way that would be opposite to what The Sinful Son would want or do. He's slowly disappearing. His body and unholy power are still here, and his anger and rage are here because they are eternal and required for powering such a monstrous entity, but the dark thoughts and desires are gone, replaced by the goodness of the artificial heart Damon has that I created to subdue my wickedness."

"Is that why you attacked the Hall of Homestead? You're trying to help people now? How?"

The blazing red eyes, which burned brighter and deadlier than before, shifted up and down as Damon nodded his head. *"Indeed. There was a girl who, by undeniable coincidence or fate, bumped into The Torturer in the street. Telling her story, we found out what was truly going on at her home, and I went to go take care of it. It was only recently that I acquired the cloak of darkness, the exosuit of power, and the eyes of condemnation, so many of our missions were marked as regular kidnappings or murders. Therefore, I assure you that the number of people I have had to fight and slaughter is far greater than anyone knows or could imagine. Luckily, The Torturer is a genius, just as I am, both criminally and detective-wise, and so, we have never been caught or even suspected. Lately, however, it's been about publicity and making a statement. I'm going to get caught or die one day, but I'm fighting and saving until the very end. I shall be the figure I always hoped would come and save Damon, allowing him to stay in control and live."*

"This situation is rather dodgy and mucky, as I'm torn over what to think about you, Mr. Damon. Besides that, I'm knackered from the long day I've had and partially gobsmacked at how personal you've gotten with me. Before I make a final decision and ask more questions, however, I'm curious as to what the second reason why you can't live a normal life is. After all, Damon could probably save just as many people if not more people than *The Sinful Son* by becoming a politician, starting a charity, or doing-"

"Thoughts such as those have crossed my mind over a thousand times, both plainly and in rhyme. However, such ideas are impossible to achieve, and they grow farther away from reality as we speak."

The red eyes disappeared, and the whole room was black again except for the small area of light around Sir Thomas. He heard heavy thuds against the ground where the eyes had just been. Unsure and growing a bit fearful, he gulped. "What are you doing?"

"I'm stripping down to nothing but my black pants, socks, and metal boots, and soon you shall see that The Sinful Son and I are truly merged together now. He is more than just a uniform. He is an idea. A belief. A person. The original. We are one and two together

and separate. Be grateful in every fiber of your heart, for only The Torturer has seen my human form. I have not been seen in public since I was eighteen. Witness the blazing sun hidden within the black hole known as my life. " As he took off his vantablack cloak, high-tech shades, and exosuit, Damon removed the voice filter mask from around his mouth, which also prevented him from being affected by his chemicals. Even without it, however, his voice was still powerfully frightening, like the roaring of an unstoppable train in a dark tunnel. "I have the mind of an *angel,* the heart of a *human,* the body of a *demon,* and the power of a *god.*"

His footsteps still heavy and menacing, Damon walked forward like a brute on his way to kill, or rather a hunter on his way toward a dying animal he had injured, ready to claim what was rightfully his. The aura exuding from him seem to disintegrate everything around him, clearing the way for the ultimate being. He stopped walking after stepping into the outermost edge of the white light around Sir Thomas, revealing his human form as he became entirely visible.

Sir Thomas almost fainted from shock. "Bollocks," he managed to mutter forcefully as he struggled to think. Every fiber, every cell, and every atom in his mortal being trembled. He did not know what to think. He did not know how to feel. He did not even know how to breathe.

Damon chuckled, the ominous notes echoing both sorrowfully and wrathfully throughout the darkness of the room. "Your reaction, which is utter speechlessness and almost tears leaking from your eyes as every cell in your body trembles, is not one that surprises me at all. Though you are only the second to see my human form, I am well aware of the effect it has on the eyes and minds of others, for it is truly unimaginable and unexpected. Do you understand now? We are one and two together. Damon and ***The Sinful Son*** stand before you, and this is why I continue on as I do, for there is nothing else I have to or can do to help. There is no saving me, but I shall gladly sacrifice myself for others. Never forget that before I was ***The Sinful Son,*** I was

The Sinless Son who was selfless and more human than anyone else. Never forget that we are more than just a uniform and fancy technology. *Never forget* that the cloak and exosuit help me but are *shackles* and that my *true* power is what you see before you. I am the true unholy power that will terrorize and save countless lives."

No longer captivated by his words or voice, and recovered from the initial shock, Sir Thomas studied the figure before him. Damon was tall and towered menacingly above Sir Thomas despite the fact that he was strung up and suspended in the air. The old man's sympathetic eyes fell upon Damon's black hair first, which was almost dark enough to match his vantablack cloak. The black hair was of medium length in height and semi-short in width, and it was spiked and smooth at the same time. From there, Sir Thomas' gaze fell done and was held hostage by the vibrant, dark green eyes just two feet away from him that were filled with immeasurable sorrow and wrath. The left eye, however, suffered from a large vertical scar, and the foggy green eye seemed to see little if it could even see at all. His teeth were slightly sharper than most but other than that and his eyes, his face, with its permanently angrily-angled eyebrows and aggressive jaw muscles, seemed normal.

The rest of Damon's body, however, was far more intriguing than his menacing face. He was both grotesque and gorgeous. He was lean and built, on top of being extremely tall, maintaining a skinny figure while still being ripped muscularity in the perfect manner. Despite the lack of width and circumference of his arms and legs, his muscles seemed to be compacted and backed by emotional strength directly connected to his mind and beliefs. In every strand of muscle fiber, there was an overwhelming power of wrath, rage, hatred, and revenge, and all of his green veins, which were bulging at the perfect level of visibility, seemed to be filled with boiling blood that was far worse than lava. There almost seemed to be steam coming from his veins. Every cell of his seemingly unnatural body exuded insane amounts of unholy power and unstoppable strength.

It was not Damon's chiseled chest, his eight-pack of abs, his masculine arms, or his frightening forearms that captured Sir Thomas' attention, but instead, he was in shock and intrigued by the brand marks that covered Damon's torso and arms. On his right pec, in large letters, the phrase "THE SINFUL SON" was branded, each word slightly to the end of the word above it. Unlike the other marks, which were slightly darker than Damon's medium-caucasian skin, "THE SINFUL SON" brand had been painted or tattooed black, as far as Sir Thomas could tell. Going diagonally and angled toward his left shoulder on his lower right torso and ending on two of his lower right abs, the word "ROTTEN" was branded, and across from it, matching its design, the word "BASTARD" was branded. While they could be read individually, those two brandings could be read together as "ROTTEN BASTARD" to increase the level of insult. Those three marks were the biggest and most notable brandings, but his whole torso and arms were covered with insults, negative adjectives, and initials branded onto him.

"Oh my God! What in bloody Hell happened to you? To see such a sight before my own eyes is completely gutting! Mr. Damon, you didn't do those to yourself, did you?"

"Undoubtedly, I assume one might think that I did, but rest assured that I did not do this to myself, and I never would perform such atrocities upon myself or anyone else. Not only is branding painful, but the words and phrases upon my bodies are haunting reminders of the past that I have never forgotten about. They are stolen from the list I wrote that recorded everything my despicable family members said about or to me, and The Torturer uses that information along with branding to punish me and such. Brace yourself, for you have not seen the worst of it yet! My back, although not flat due to my muscularity, has far more room for pain."

Damon turned around, revealing a muscular back that, as he had warned, was far worse than his torso or arms. In all different sizes and at several different angles, branded words and phrases covered his flesh. There was almost no room for any more to be made.

Sir Thomas did not have time to read them all, but he skimmed the words and phrases across Damon's back and triceps, seeing: USELESS SON, UNINTELLIGENT, BUM, MORONIC, IDIOT, STUPID, LOSER, FUCKING RIDICULOUS, DISAPPOINTMENT, PIECE OF CRAP, FAILURE, SCRAWNY, WEAK, FOREVER ALONE, IMMATURE, UNSERIOUS, FUTURE-PRISONER, IMMATURE, MONSTER, DELUSIONAL, EVIL, MENTALLY-ILL, FOOL, IRRITABLE, SON-OF-A-BITCH, LIAR IRRESPONSIBLE INTROVERT, MUMBLER, COMPLAINER, FREAK, and LAZY. The largest letters made up the phrase "A FAILURE TO SOCIETY," and that was branded on his back just above his waistline. The other two major ones were up on the top of his shoulder blades, and they too were larger than the rest, angled at a slope toward each arm. On his left shoulder blade, the word "WORTHLESS" was branded, and on his right shoulder blade, the word "OUTCAST" was branded, the two words able to be read both individually and together.

Sir Thomas was speechless as Damon turned back around, his arms folded across his chest. Each breath that he took seemed vicious and filled with rage and hatred, yet there was no denying the sorrow in his eyes either. "Mr. Damon, how old are you?"

"I am approaching forty or perhaps past that point, but I do not *know*, as I stopped keeping track some time *ago*. After seeing the brands upon my *back*, why do you ask a question such as *that*?

"While I can't deny the emotions that consume your body and every feature, you only appear to be twenty or thirty at most! Perhaps your mid-twenties would be what most people would think. I thought that such anger would make you age faster than a normal human be-ing, and perhaps it has done so internally, but on the outside, you appear far younger than you actually are."

Damon laughed softly, and it was not menacing or ominous as usual, but it was human and warm. "Indeed, what you have observed is undeniably true, and I am both fortunate and unfortunate as always for the state of my body. Internally, I'm sure that my cardiovascular system has suffered greatly. After all, a human is not meant to exist in a constant state of uncontrollable rage and hatred. Anger is undoubtedly the strongest emotional fuel, matched only by love, but it is not a natural fuel for the engines of our body. What is the heart? It's the engine of the body, and constantly having such unnatural fuel run through it has damaged it, along with all of the pipes that lead from the engine to the rest of my body. However, through the unholy power of **The Sinful Son**, I have stayed a young man as best as I can in order to have the appearance, speed, intelligence, and strength necessary to complete my journey and help others. Humans grow old, deteriorate, and die, but **The Sinful Son** is a belief and almost more than human. Therefore, as supernatural as it might seem, his combination with myself has kept me young. In fact, I have watched countless shows and read countless stories in which people, who were far older than you and I, held on passionately to their youth until they accomplished their goal. They stayed young until they completed their dreams, but mine is unattainable, and I'm constantly powered by negative emotions. It seems ironic, but it keeps me young. I feel, move, and believe that I'm in my twenties."

"I understand, and I'm impressed by such a feat, but why maintain such a perfect body only to have The Torturer ruin it? Why would you allow that."

Damon stepped backward and disappeared into the darkness. "I won't deny that my relationship with her is toxic and troubled." He put back on the unholy garments of **The Sinful Son**, and the red eyes reappeared in the darkness, though they did not burn as angrily as before. "***It is a horrible existence, and I should have left her long ago, but how could I, a person more human than anyone, abandon her? Besides that, I do love her. I always have, though, that love has been on the decline recently. She's a manipulator and an evil woman, but there's good in her. I know it. I love it. She needs me. How could I ever abandon a person who needs my help, let alone the woman I love and have been with for so long. She needs my help. I want-***"

"I don't need *anyone*," a feminine voice stated coldly from across the room. Sir Thomas and Damon looked toward the entrance of the room as the bland lights turned on, revealing the woman descending the staircase behind him. "Your task was to capture the geezer and tie him up for me. I never said anything about spending your time talking to him, nor did I give you permission to discuss our personal relationship."

The towering menace swiftly turned around, his cloak flying up into the air, his back to Sir Thomas, as Damon looked at the woman, who was slowly approaching him. "*That is true, but it is also undeniably true that I don't need your permission to discuss anything about my personal life with anyone, Francesca. I am the one who decides what to do with my life, just as I have ever since that day when I resurrected. You may have saved me and brought me back to life, but that doesn't mean you own me. I've repaid my debt to you a thousand times more than necessary. At the same time, I shall let you know that you're not in charge here. Not only are we supposed to be a couple outside of our unholy tasks, but we're also co-founders of this operation. Also, he's not a geezer. You are to respect him, as he is wise and kind, and he has nothing to do with us at all. I don't know why you insisted on capturing him or what you plan on using him for, but I shall not allow you to harm him. In fac-*" Damon stopped talking as Francesca stood up on her toes and hugged him.

"I know all of that, and I thought you realized that I had changed after yesterday," Francesca said seductively with hurt feelings and innocence. "Didn't we snuggle? I let that guy live, didn't I? Things are changing, and so are we. Isn't that what you want?"

"*Of course that's what I want for us both, for it's-*"

From behind her angel-wing-scarred back in a bag, Francesca whipped out a branding gun with the metal letters "F.L." on the end. She smashed the metal letters, which were both one inch tall, into the left side of Damon's neck, burning him. "*I am* in charge here, Damon, and don't forget that." **The Sinful Son** roared monstrously as he grabbed his neck, placing the cold metal of the gloves against the burning flesh. "Sex, flirtations, and humoring you with the idea of love are all special privileges you get, but your behavior lately appalls me, so now I have to punish you. I can't believe you fell for that! Get the fuck out of here."

"Bloody Hell!" Sir Thomas was shocked at the fighting between his two captors, and now he knew that The Torturer would show him no mercy. This was his chance to have Damon help him escape. "Don't just stand there and take it, Mr. Damon! Attack that crazy bitch! You shouldn't allow her to hurt you just because you love her."

Francesca laughed maniacally. "Stay out of this, old bastard," she snapped as she stormed toward Sir Thomas, a wicked grin on her pale face. She instantly stopped just a few feet away from him when Damon's left hand fell upon her left shoulder, and a feeling of utter death filled the room.

The Sinful Son towered menacingly behind the frail Francesca, his right hand still against his neck where he had just been branded. His body, despite how many times it had been branded, had not entirely grown used to such an unnatural feeling. While he was not bothered by it too much, it was not something insignificant, especially since Francesca increased the heat every time, knowing that Damon was more than capable of brushing off such major injuries. The pain was unbearable, but he used the unholy power of living the past while simultaneously living the present to fill himself with unfathomable anger that surpassed the pain he was feeling. Every major disagreement and argument that he had ever had with Francesca played through his mind, pouring out of his broken heart. He held on to her left shoulder tightly, as a warning, and she stood there in front of him, motionless and silent. "***Francesca, that man is right in telling me that I should attack and snap your back in half, but I shall not harm you. I respect women, and hurting them even when attacked is not something I entirely agree with, though you have done more than just attack me. Either way, my love for you is greater than my unstoppable hate and***

rage, for you are all that I have and want. I know that I cannot live a normal life. Neither of us can, but at-"

"I don't need to hear you lecture me again," Francesca stated coldly but with honesty, still facing Sir Thomas, not turning around to face the monster behind her. "We go over this all the time, and it's always the same conversation, but nothing *ever* changes. I *can't* change, Damon, and I don't know why you don't understand that by now. Maybe *you* can change, and it seems like you already have just from talking to that old-fart and yourself, but I'm *not* going to change. I admire the fact that you've been so adaptable and selfless in life, but it's because I'm the opposite of those things. You *think* you're a savior, and maybe you actually are one, but there's no saving me. *We're over*, Damon. You always state that I'm a manipulator and a liar, but you never actually believe it enough to get it through your head. It's bullshit to say you overlook those things because they can't be overlooked."

"Do not speak in haste during a state of mental unclarity and-"

"I *mean* it, Damon! I stopped loving you a long time ago, and I never truly loved you anyway, because I can't love. You say that you're more human than anyone, but that doesn't make up for or cancel out my lack of humanity. My mind, heart, and soul are tainted and wicked because I am crazy and sadistic. I live off of the pain of others, and so, I must live alone to stop myself from hurting others. You can keep that stupid outfit, but leave this place and take that rotten brat with you. She's annoying me, just as you are. I have no need for you. You're obsolete compared to the power of that speedster. That's why I had you go fight him. I want him to be the new you because *The Sinful Son* is no longer a part of my life, nor is he necessary for my future plans. He's nothing but an old ghost story told around campfires, and people barely do that anymore. So, yes, I might be casting you out like everyone else has, but I know that you can survive and handle such treatment."

"Francesca Leach, how dare you speak to me like this at a time so crucial to our lives and in the presence of an outsider. I think that

simply throwing me away today will not change anything or make your life better. You and I should have one final talk in great length and detail regarding everything, and we can plan the future from there. I was born evil, overcame it with goodness, was turned evil, and then was transformed into a being of two evils and one good, but Francesca, I shall die a good man, and you shall die a good woman. You can be saved and helped."

"Don't you *get* it, Damon? *This is* our final talk, and that's why you've said less than you ever have before because the final talk is meant to be blunt and direct. There's no more trying to fix our relationship or ourselves because both are too far gone. No amount of poetry or rhyming can persuade me. I *don't* want to be saved or helped. In fact, I *like* being The Torturer. I love and enjoy it! It physically brings me joy, and mentally, I have grown to love living life with no morals, doing as I please. So, if you want to overpower '*The Sinful Son*' with 'Damon' and his beliefs, go for it, but you *won't* stop me from doing what I want. Now, remove your hand from my shoulder before I go crazy."

"Of course, I shall do so promptly. First, however, I-"

"I said unhand me and leave," Francesca screeched, her face a vile disfigurement of emotions. "I'm in charge here, and I hate you!" Throwing the branding gun to the ground, she instantly whipped out a unique knife with her right hand, and Sir Thomas recognized its remarkable design, as it was his Deconstructor Blade.

"Blimey! Mr. Damon, look out," Sir Thomas yelled as a warning, as he pulled against the ropes, but it was too late.

Elegantly spinning around, with a powerful strike, Francesca sliced through Damon's left arm with the knife, severing it halfway up his forearm. His hand and the attached piece of arm fell to the ground with a heavy thud as the metal hit the cement floor. Bright red blood gushed out from the wound, and it was so red that one would not think it to be human blood, but rather it looked like lava or a solar flare. As the hot liquid collided with the ground, it seemed to form steam and corrode the cement.

Combined with the ability to break apart atomic bonds, the sharp blade had cut so cleanly through the metal and Damon's flesh, that there was almost no pain. Rather, his savage roar seemed to be one of revenge and wrath instead of sorrow and pain. Seeing that Francesca was still armed with the fatal weapon, and knowing that he had to attend to his injury right away, Damon had no choice but to swiftly depart, almost flying away like a phantom as he ran up the staircase toward the exit with incredible speed. He stopped in the dark doorway, towering and ominous, seemingly more monstrous than ever before. ***"I'll be back to rescue you, old man, and I shall personally end your miserable life and reign of terror, Francesca,"*** Damon stated determinedly before disappearing. His words could almost be heard around the entire globe.

"We'll see about that," Francesca yelled at the empty doorway. She turned around and walked toward Sir Thomas, grinning maliciously. "He's really got me all emotional and crazy now, so I might not be able to control myself. I'm on the edge of bursting with the desire to torture and kill. Of course, I'll try my best *not* to kill you. After all, there's a lot I need from you. Either way, it seems like it's just you and me now, so let's get started."

CHAPTER 3

THE FLIGHT TO GO FIGHT

(Charleston, West Virginia. The Same Day: April 18, 2022)

Stepping outside, Birch filled his giant lungs with a deep breath before slowly exhaling the crisp morning air, experiencing a kind of bitter peace that could only be achieved when one accepted the inevitable. After being contacted by Abraham once more, he knew that today was the day he would travel to England to face off against the madman who destroyed his gym and posed a threat to the world greater than nuclear weapons ever had.

The gentle spring breeze flowed over Birch's bald head and past the graphene area of his shoulder as he walked toward the cattle pen. He had woken up early as always, suffering from another sleepless night and rolling out of bed with the sun. Before he could leave for England, and uncertain of how long he would be gone for, Birch needed to prepare the animals for one of his tenants to take care of while he was gone. He had tried contacting Michael but had been unable to reach him for the past few days.

Tired from all of the morning farm work, Birch retreated into his old house to relax before he left for the rendevous point in just an hour. He strolled into his living room, plopping down with a soft thud on a red couch that was against the back wall. To his left sat a fish tank with a few goldfish. Birch turned his head and stared at the small fish. *Can't say I'm not anxious about the future. What if I get shot through the chest with that gun? Look at muh shoulduh. I might die tuhday, and that's uh scary thought. I may be an outcast, but I love life. It's uhmazing, and it's awful that so many take it fuh granted. I still got people tuh help, but if possibly sacrificin' muhself tuhday will ensure the safety of the future, muh giant back is more than willin' tuh carry the burden fuh everyone.* Birch looked at the fish as they darted here and there or slowly swam by. *Y'all have it easy, don't ya? Swimmin' around with nothin' tuh worry about. I'm uh bit envious, though I know it ain't entirely easy either. I s'pose we've all got our own troubles and worries, don't we?* Birch sighed.

Trying not to think and worry too much, Birch tried to meditate, though he had never been good at the practice. He fell asleep, and the crushing duties of reality pressed into his mind, forming a horrific nightmare of what the future might hold. In this imaginary world made by his subconscious, Birch was out working on the farm. It was a regular day, and after a while, he decided to take a break. Taking a stroll into the woods, he walked along a dirt path as the fictional Virginian sun beat down on his bald head, much hotter than usual. Birch became drenched with sweat, and he wiped his brow, fearing the wrathful sting of the droplets should they slip into his eyes. It was sweltering hot, and his vision was not entirely clear, as the heat distorted the air, bending it and making it wavy.

Birch peered down the dirt path lined with trees, something catching his attention. In the distance, Michael was hanging from the limb of a birch tree, a noose around his neck. He was desperately grasping at the rope, struggling to breathe and live. Instinctively, Birch started running toward Michael to try and save him, but he could not run any faster than a baby could crawl. Without a vibration of warning, the dirt below started engulfing Birch's body as if it were quicksand. He sunk down into the coarse soil, struggling to get out. Green vines, both thick and thin, burst out from the ground and wrapped around his monstrous arms. He could not break free from their grasp as they began to drag him deeper into the earth. As the dirt concealed Birch's face, there was nothing left uncovered but his one eye. He saw a figure, and he cried out for their help, but his heart sunk when he recognized the attire the figure wore as the standard uniform of a member of The Organization. They smirked before kicking dirt over the last visible part of him, burying Birch alive in the fictional landscape.

Birch woke up, startled by the nightmare and gasping for air, sweating as his body ached. He looked around, slowly steadying his breathing, making sure that The Organization was not in that very room watching him. As he scanned the room, his eyes lingered and went back to the time on the clock as he realized that he had to go soon.

Not wishing to leave his custom-made convertible at the rendevous point, Birch had decided that he would walk to where they were all supposed to be meeting. He chugged down one of his plant-shakes to get his body up and running. Packing a bag, Birch made sure to include two gallons of water, a variety of granola bars, and other basic travel goods, as he was unsure of what The Organization would provide and whether or not they could be trusted.

Before he left, Birch turned around and took a good look at the farm, his home, and everything else he was temporarily leaving behind, or perhaps, permanently leaving behind. He studied everything carefully, afraid that this might be the last time he saw all of this. Birch looked at his shoulder. The slick surface almost glowed in the sunlight in an unnatural and unsettling way. He rubbed his left hand over it, slowly, feeling the difference between it and his skin, and reminding himself why he had to do what he was going to do. Birch was not a killer. It haunted him, the question of why Kronos had destroyed his gym, but in his heart, he did know that the gym was just a building that could be rebuilt. He would not deny that revenge burned within his heart, but it was currently outshined by his determination to prevent such devastation from affecting the lives of others.

After walking for almost two hours, the sun was just an hour away from noon as Birch arrived at the coordinates that Abraham had given him. It was a clear pasture filled with relatively tall grass. In the midst of it stood a huge private plane and a solid black car with tinted windows. Abraham got out of the passenger side of the vehicle. For the faint second that the car door had been open, Birch caught a glimpse of the woman who had been driving the car. She, like all the members of the organization, was dressed in black business attire with black shades. Abraham, on the other hand, had no shades and wore a grey suit. Birch assumed that it must have indicated that he was of higher authority than the rest of them.

Following Abraham, Birch walked up the large ramp that led into the back of the plane. He glanced over his fixed shoulder, noting that the car was still there, the woman watching him. It slowly turned away before speeding off down the field.

"Don't worry about her, Mr. Willow," Abraham reassured. "She was just my ride here, and it's only right that she makes sure I got onto the plane safely."

"Of course," Birch replied neutrally with a nod of his head. "I don't trust any o' ya, tuh be honest, but I'll ruhspect the rules and way of doin' things that you people have amongst yourselves. That's only fair, and since you're providin' me with everything I need, I'll be compliant with your rules. I'm uh peaceful man who don't seek no trouble. However, know that tuh stab uh knife in muh back is futile since the blade is unable tuh pierce through muh thick muscles if ya understand the analogy I'm making. I'd hate tuh have tuh rip it out and throw it away, or even worse, use it against those who wielded it."

"Yes, of course, Mr. Willow. There's no need for you to warn us at all, as The Organization is aware of the power you possess and how dangerous you can be if provoked, so we intend on maintaining peace with you. I assure you that we're both on the same side here. This isn't a scheme to try and get your research and whether you believe that or not is entirely up to you. I don't mean to insult you or your intelligence, but atomic weaponry is far superior to being able to digest plants more efficiently. I'm not discrediting your research, as it is remarkable, but it's in the shadow of a breakthrough beyond all science."

"Hmph. Such is life." Birch looked at the size of the plane as they finished climbing the ramp. "This is uh massive plane for just us, don't ya think?"

Abraham slapped Birch on the back in a friendly manner. "Well, you're a big man, Mr. Willow. Speaking of that, I have something I'd like to show you over here. Some of our elite blacksmiths and nerds were working on these for you," Abraham bragged as he gestured over to the left wall of the plane in front of them.

The wall consisted of two indented spaces, which were used to display armors. There were two sets of complete armor. One of them was white and black, matching the pattern of a birch tree, and the other was grey and had light green lines and engravements all across it, matching the appearance of a willow tree.

Birch studied everything quickly, not thrilled by what he saw. "Pfft. These are fuh me? You intend on havin' me fight 'em in uh suit of armor like I'm uh knight or some fictional character? Ya even had 'em designed tuh look like the trees o' my name. What's this *nonsense*, Abraham? Ya can't be serious."

"We are serious, and I assure you that these are not rusty pieces of armor that we dug out of some ancient graves. These are high-tech sets of armor designed to be bulletproof, resistant to fire, and resistant to electrical currents. Those are basic and won't do too much when you're facing atomic weaponry, but it'll help."

"I have uh lot tuh say tuh that, but I'll just let it go. None of it really matters at the end of the day, so no point in arguin' ov'r it. If I do wear one of those, it'll be the willow one, as the birch armor resembles uh cow too much." Birch turned and faced Abraham, his expression harsh and cold. He towered over the regular man, and he seemed bigger and more muscular than ever. It seemed as if even bullets could not pierce his giant muscles. "However, before anythin' else happens, we have tuh establish trust, which means you have tuh tell me the truth." Birch looked past Abraham as the ramp to the plane closed, and two agents appeared, each of them armed with a pistol, a taser, and a knife.

"Of course, Mr. Willow. We believe in trust, and we *are* allies, so feel free to ask your questions. I understand that you probably have a lot going through your mind right now. I won't be able to give you information that's been classified by our leader, but you're welcome to ask about anything concerning you regarding this mission."

Birch looked down at Abraham, his face stern and determined to find out the truth. "What happened tuh Michael Kellson? I haven't heard from him in days now, and I know that he's not ignorin' me. He ain't that kind o' person. What exactly did The Organization do tuh him?"

"I have no idea, Mr. Willow," Abraham replied as he shrugged his shoulders. "Mr. Kellson has nothing to do with us or our mission, and I assure you that-"

"I wasn't asking, Abraham," Birch stated firmly. The two agents came closer. "I'm demanding tuh know because he's gone, and I will tear this whole place apart as well as The Organization if you guys killed him fuh knowin' anything. He's an innocent civilian who has nothin' tuh do with any of this."

"That's mutiny and conspiracy against The Organization," one of the agents declared as he shot his taser into Birch's chest, right where his scars were.

The giant was completely unaffected by the high voltage of the taser, despite the fact that the current was being sent directly into his chest. Birch's face hardened as he grabbed the cords with his bare hand and yanked the taser away from the agent, throwing it to the side as he took a powerful step forward. "That won't work, son. You best get out of here before I show ya how real men settle their differences, and I definitely won't be the usual pacifist I am." The two agents drew their pistols and swiftly came to either side of Abraham. "Oh? How laughable. I don't think even uh shotgun blast could stop me or muh muscles," Birch stated boldly as he cracked his powerful knuckles.

"At ease, gentleman," Abraham commanded. "There's no need for any violence aboard this plane. Mr. Willow's curiosity is understandable." The two agents reluctantly put their guns away. "I have no idea what happened to him. I did have an agent speak with Mr. Kellson about joining our team for a high-paying position since he knew about us. We could use a scientific mind like his, after all, and he'd be safer working with us than on his own in the shadows. That was the last any of us saw of him, and we'll attempt contacting him again soon enough. Believe it or not, I have a feeling that he'll join our team of geniuses. He'd fit right in."

"Hmph." Birch looked at the two agents and smirked. "I'll let it go, for now, as we have an important mission tuh do. Just know that if you're lying, you'll pay fuh it one day, whether it's by my giant hand or someone else's. That's all."

Abraham led the way, answering his phone, talking non-stop to several different people. Birch used this to his advantage as he took a good look around the interior plane. He wanted to be ready for anything. The cargo bay he was in was massive, matching the size of the private aircraft. In it were two vehicles, scraped and scratched up, the paint chipped in certain areas. One of them had snow dripping off of it, and the other was splashed with mud. He assumed the vehicles had been used just recently, as the stains were fresh. Squinting through the tinted glass, he saw the faint outline of what appeared to be various animals. They were either tranquilized or dead, for they were almost completely still, as far as he could tell.

Abraham noticed that Birch was checking out the vehicles, and so he stopped walking and put his phone away. "I see you've taken an interest in our cleanup program, Mr. Willow. It makes sense since you love animals, and I'm sure you're curious about this huge plane and what we use it for. In fact, The Organization would love for you to help us out with our cleanup program once you're done with this mission. We already know that you're good with bears."

Birch was mildly curious but mostly suspicious of the so-called cleanup program. "I think I might pass, but let's not get ahead of ourselves here. One mission at uh time. What exactly is this cleanup program?"

"It's a wonderful program, in my opinion. It helps people while also greatly boosting the positive reputation of The Organization for the day we come out of the shadows. We don't do it here in the States, however. We usually prefer to help out with third-world countries. We get the animals out of the streets, yards, homes, and wherever else they may be. They include roadkill and live animals that pose a danger to families and people."

"I would agree that it's uh wonderful program, as it does sound great, but I do have uh concern."

"Figures you would, Mr. Willow, given how caring you are when it comes to nature. Rest assured that the live animals are tranquilized and released in a safe environment that they can thrive in without harming the balance already there. In fact, they go to our Artificial Island Rejuvenation Project."

"Good. What about these crates everywhere? What does G.C. stand for?" Birch was gesturing to a bunch of crates, boxes, and containers labeled with the abbreviation G.C. on them. They were scattered all over the cargo bay, many of them being identified with warning labels. "Are those the letters for the new name of The Organization soon tuh be released tuh the public or whatever?"

"Precisely so, Mr. Willow. If everything goes well on this mission, we should be coming out of the shadows soon, and it's thanks to your assistance. Now, on with the tour. This plane is designed so you can move freely about when flying, but we have a room prepared for you so you can relax before the confrontation. Follow me right this way, Mr. Willow," Abraham commanded with a wave as he began to ascend up a large staircase that led to a second level in the plane.

There was a small scientific lab in between the cargo bay and the main rooms of the plane, and Birch tried to look at everything without getting caught. There were large flat screen computers, but none of them were on. Birch had to turn his body in order to fit through this narrow area. He used this to his advantage. When he rotated his body, Birch pretended to have accidentally bumped his waist into one of the desks. The mouse moved, and Birch hoped that it might wake the computer up from sleeping mode, but it was of no use. The computers were turned off. The Organization did not want him seeing what they were up to. He looked around at everything else. There were syringes filled with strange liquids, tranquilizer darts, and strange parts, but nothing out of the ordinary for a company doing a cleanup project or scientific research.

"Come now, follow me right this way, Mr. Willow." Abraham made a few turns down the metal grate path they were on, and they left the lab area. They entered into an open space in the plane, plenty wide and high for Birch. It was a fancy room, and golden streams of sunlight flooded into it, basking everything in its warming light. There were a few small windows on the left side of the room right above a velvet sofa. Birch sat down on the expensive furniture and looked through one of the windows. The land below was just a blanket of green that slowly got less and less out of focus. They were already ascending, and he had not even noticed.

"This plane is completely silent," Birch commented as he turned away from the window. "It's also very balanced and stable. I'm quite impressed."

"Ah, thank you, Mr. Willow. We have some of the top minds here at The Organization. They were born for their passions, and so we employ them. They work for us, and in return, they receive a considerable profit. I must attend to the pilots. I'll check in on you later. We should be there in just a few hours. We'll make it just before they do."

"*What?*" Birch clenched his giant hands into fists. "What do you mean by that? You know where they are?"

"Of course. We know *everything*, Mr. Willow. Our agents had been tracking them in Minnesota, where there were rumors of a vigilante with the power to run at superhuman speeds and manipulate the forces of time, or at least people's perception of time. From what we know, that vigilante has allied themselves with Sir Thomas and Kronos, and the three of them were traveling together for over a day to get to Florida. Along the way, they stopped at several places to rest, and at one of them, they ate at Dr. Finch's Fast Food. The franchise was created by Dr. Finch, who also happens to be a prominent member of The Organization."

"Then why didn't you stop them? That's complete-"

"Calm yourself, Mr. Willow. They were heading to Florida to confront a man known as *The Sinful Son*. He's a terrorist-like figure we've been tracking for a while. Like all people, we hoped to kill two birds with one stone by allowing Kronos to take care of *The Sinful Son* for us instead of losing several agents in the fight. *The Sinful Son* is dangerous, and I rather have more capable individuals deal with him then our ill-equipped agents. We did lose one agent today during their confrontation, but it was a necessary sacrifice."

"What do ya mean? Kronos, Sir Thomas, and this vigilante guy with powers fought *The Sinful Son* tuhday?"

"Yes, and it was just a few hours ago. Early this morning, they confronted *The Sinful Son* and then they all vanished somewhere in the ocean shortly after. An agent posing as a police officer was sent there ahead of time to capture footage, but he was killed during the battle, which was quite intense compared to normal fights in our society. He managed to film some of it before being taken out. We had hoped he could escape, but, unfortunately, he did not. Take a look at this footage," Abraham said as he gestured to a television on the other side of the room, ten feet away from them. "It's actually on the news everywhere now, but the video sent into the news from bystanders was poor quality. So is the footage that our agent captured, but he was actually involved and up close."

Using his phone, Abraham turned on the television and played the footage he had received from the agent. Birch watched attentively, interested in the fight amongst individuals that were above regular humans. He had not entirely believed Kronos, who had told him that such people existed, but if The Organization was searching as hard as Kronos was, Birch figured the rumors must be true. After all, he, himself, was quite extraordinary. The screen was dark as the sky above raged with a storm, and as black smoke clouded the streets, growing worse as the video progressed. Amongst this darkness, Birch could only see one thing. It was something big, moving like a shadow from spot to spot. The figure looked almost as tall as him. Lights flashed here and there as rain fell down. A pair of red eyes stared at the camera and flashed forward at the agent before the footage was cut out. The sounds were gruesome.

"Hmm. Well, that's somethin' new. I don't believe in fairies or anything, but that was certainly uh monster of some kind. That black smoke that was all o'er the street was his doing?"

"Indeed, Mr. Willow. I'm sure you can understand why he was a concern of ours. Anyway, he disappeared somewhere in the ocean near Florida, and so did the trio of troublemakers that you have to deal with. So, that's why we were not engaging with them just yet. However, we expect that they will head back to England once they are done dealing with their problems over by Florida. Since we don't know whether they'll return home, go to a secret base, or go to their store, we're going to drop you onto their main store to destroy it, just as they destroyed your gym, and then they'll have no choice but to show up where you are to try and stop you. That's when you'll take them on, and then we'll back you up with agents from a distance. We'll be on standby and then have the whole area swarmed in a minute."

"That's fine and all, but what about **The Sinful Son**? I wasn't prepared tuh fight the livin' embodiment o' death or anything. What do ya guys know about him? I assume that he won't be joinin' 'em, but it don't hurt tuh be prepared."

"He's difficult to follow and track, and his 'boss' is even more tricky to study and predict, but we have enough intel to give you a basic idea. Most importantly: understand that he *is* human, and at most, he's just a skilled illusionist. He's quite monstrous, but he is *not* a monster.

He uses a variety of science and technology to manipulate the senses, change his person, and exaggerate his factors of intimidation to create fear. Besides that, he uses chemical weaponry. We also know that he's very tall, and we estimate him to be a little over seven feet tall. Not all of his height is natural, and he's still almost a foot shorter than you are, but he *is* tall. The combination of his natural and technological strength is phenomenal, and it may even match yours. We're not entirely sure."

"Hmph. That's uh bit concerning, quite honestly. Fightin' against atomic weaponry and Kronos was already uh lot tuh handle. He caught me off guard at the gym when we fought the other day, but it wasn't just that. He was just clownin' around, and it wasn't because he was arrogant. It was because he was powerful, and he proved that he's much more than just his weapons and gadgets. He's uh complete genius, and his body is almost unnatural. Holdin' my own against 'im in addition tuh uh vigilante who can manipulate time and move super fast, while also fightin' off someone almost as big and as strong as me, who also has crazy tech, ain't goin' tuh be easy. In fact, it might be impossible. I wasn't signin' up for uh suicide-mission, Abraham. I signed up tuh stop madmen with dangerous weapons from goin' 'round and ruinin' people's lives."

"Still humble as always, I see. You should be more confident in both your own powers as well as my army of agents. However, you shouldn't worry about **The Sinful Son** that much. As far as we know, he was most likely killed by the D.O.O.M. Shooter or something else, so there's no need to worry about him." Abraham's phone vibrated in his pocket, and he answered it, turning away from Birch. "He left Cape Cod?" He nodded his head. "Perfect… yes… hold on for one second." Abraham turned toward Birch, holding his phone away. "If you'll excuse me, Mr. Willow, I have some important matters to take care of. Work has been extra busy this past week. It's going to be a long ride but faster than any plane could get to England. Enjoy the flight." Abraham did a fake salute before turning away to head for a door. He left through it and followed a hallway into the cockpit of the plane.

Birch sighed. "Ain't life turnin' out tuh be somethin' truly bizarre? I s'pose I brought this all tuh muhself. Either way, I guess I'm headin' tuh England to fight some crazy individuals."

CHAPTER 4

RESCUE MISSION

(Homestead, Florida. That Same Day: April 18, 2022.)

With each passing second, Sir Thomas grew more fearful that Kronos and Timothy would be too late to save him. Francesca had left the room to put away the branding gun, which she had made herself, and to get changed into a more pleasant outfit, according to her. He doubted, however, that she was also putting away the Deconstructor Blade she had stolen from him. He anxiously waited in the room, tied up as he was, hoping that Damon would return before she did.

"I'm back!" Francesca exclaimed happily with sadistic joy as she descended the staircase into the torture chamber, making her way across the room to where Sir Thomas was. "Don't worry, old man… I'm *totally* fine now. Phew, man. Damon certainly got me acting a bit crazy, but I'll be sane for a while." Her tone shifted to a colder one as her eyes narrowed. "After all, conversing with you is an important part of my grand plan. You have a lot of information that I need to know. Start by introducing yourself."

"Well, Ms. Leach, perhaps if I were not tied up, I would bow. Then I could properly introduce myself, or I could kneel down and kiss the top of your hand like a gentleman."

Francesca grinned and laughed crazily at his remark. "Wow. You've got some big balls for an old man, talking to me like that. I do like the flattery, however, and I can't get enough of it. In fact, I read a whole book on flattery once. See, your flattering is from fear and is mostly false, unlike Damon's, which is real and annoying." She smirked mischievously at him. "I think we're going to have a lot of fun with this. Continue on. I want to know *all* about you and your science."

"Of course. I am Sir Thomas, son of-"

Francesca broke out cackling. "That's so odd! *Sir* Thomas? Wait, are you like a knight or something? I mean, you *are* from England, right?" She put a hand over her mouth. "I'm so sorry. That was like racist or something. Or is stereotypical the proper term? Are you going to behead me for that, *Sir* Thomas?"

Sir Thomas sighed and pretended to sob. "Blimey! I don't know how or why Mr. Damon puts up with you. I'm already knackered from talking to you, and most of what you say is rubbish. I'm afraid I haven't been knighted, as that is now a rare occasion and an old tradition that has almost been forgotten. Being called Sir Thomas is a bit fancier than being called Mr. Thomas, but it's not too different. It's just a title I have as a gentleman and a caretaker."

"Woah. I didn't realize British people had fancy stuff in even their names too. That's crazy overboard. Anyway, none of that matters. Shall we get down to business? My life may consist of doing nothing all day except for one torture session at minimum, but I'll have you know that my time is precious. As important as you are, I don't want to waste all day chatting away with you."

"I assure the feeling is mutual. I have tea to get to, as well as two nerds to attend to. Someone is going to have to clean up their mess, and I know neither of them will."

"Mmm. Now that we've gotten that out of the way, I think perhaps we should get to know each other a bit." Francesca laughed warmly, humming internally rather than letting the noise out. She rubbed the underside of Sir Thomas' chin, and he quickly pulled his head away in response. The back of his head smashed into the wall behind him, and he winced in pain.

"That looked and sounded like it hurt, quite a bit," Francesca said psychotically as she licked her lips. "No blood, but that was still *soooooo* satisfying for me.

"My God," Sir Thomas muttered as the life drained from him. He looked at Francesca, realizing that her humanity was close to the border between good and evil, if not just beyond it. "Look at your face! You really do thrive on the pain of others, and that wicked smile says it all."

"Of course, I do," Francesca hissed. "Why would Damon or I lie about something like that? I *torture* people because I'm addicted, and I love it! I get such a feeling out of it. It's why I'm a genius because it allows me to invent new weapons that'll give me even more pleasure by torturing people differently, more painfully, or more slowly. It's no exaggeration, old man. I'll actually start to get withdrawal. I may be insane, but I except it and love it."

"I figured you were a genius. After all, you created the gear and chemicals for **The Sinful Son** to use. You made him your personal weapon by manipulating him emotionally, which was and is his major weakness, then combined it with your deadly inventions. What kind of weapons could you possibly invent to make pain all the worse? Why not use that talent to help out militaries or vigilantes? To use a gift so selfishly as you have is unforgivable!"

Francesca laughed maniacally. "*Oh*, you would *not* believe the stuff I've invented!" She got intimately close to Sir Thomas" face. "I'm much more than just a pretty face. I'm insane and lack morals, so I assure you that my genius has never been wrongfully chained down like most people's intelligence because of society. Using my personal gift that's meant for me isn't selfish at all, you caring bastard. Our talents are ultimately for us and our survival and prosperity. It's only out of the goodness of our hearts that we feel obligated to share them with others, and that privilege had become an expectation rather than something people appreciate. So, I'll use my gift for myself only. I'm always tinkering. You should see the storage room and the secret basement I have. Guns, swords, axes, saws, and every type of weapon you could think of, all modified to bring out the maximum level of pain. Not just weapons but tools as well." She switched to whispering romantically to him. "See, once I torture someone one way, it doesn't make me happy if I do it again. So, for years and all time to come, I have to constantly find new ways to inflict pain. It's the worse curse anyone could bestow upon me. I can never find joy in the same type of torturing? That complicates things. Otherwise, I'll truly go insane. Can you blame me? It's not selfish. It's choosing to survive rather than be locked away or die."

"Is that so? I still don't agree with it."

Francesca backed away from her victim and pulled out what looked like a remote. "Here, check this out." As she pushed a button on the remote, a rectangular part of the floor opened up in the back corner of the room to the left of Sir Thomas. "I'm not lying, so take a look for yourself and understand that I *need* to live, and to live, I must torture."

Sir Thomas screamed in shock at what he saw. Francesca turned her attention away from him and looked over at the device that had been raised out of the ground on a platform where the floor had opened up. She broke out laughing. "Oh God, I meant to clean that up. I'm so sorry you had to see that. I meant for you to just see the device. I forgot that I never got rid of the body."

The device striking terror into the heart of Sir Thomas was a guillotine, but instead of just chopping off the head, it was longways, splitting the body in half down the spine. There was a limp corpse cut in two, still underneath the blade. Blood was stained everywhere, and rotten clumps of human organs had been spilled out of the man whose skin was turning grey and deteriorating. Francesca pushed a button on the remote, and the guillotine and platform retreated back into hiding underneath the floor.

"Bloody Hell! I'm going to chunder! How could you *forget* about something like that?" Sir Thomas asked in shock.

"Yeesh. That's a bit embarrassing. Well, after so many victims, you start to lose track," Francesca replied casually. "That, and I've been busy with Damon and the whole speedster situation. That guy's dead, though, so who actually cares? That corpse wasn't bothering anyone, and that's the benefit of having torture devices that go back underground when you're not using them. You should've seen the people I had strung up the other day. They were *way* worse than that guy."

"That's sickening," Sir Thomas spat out. "Have you no morality or compassion? Do you not value human life? Granted, you shouldn't torture animals either, but that would be preferable. I mean, all of these people have families and lives. Some of them are still young, are they not?"

"Sickening? Perhaps, but not as disturbing as what this machine can do!" Francesca pushed a button on the remote, and a rectangular platform opened up in the other corner of the room, horizontally across from where the guillotine had appeared. "I call this brutal machine, Sensory-Overloader. Not my favorite and I was rather disappointed by the effects. The pain was more mental for the victim, I suppose, and that doesn't bring me as much pleasure. Of course, I've invented hundreds of different devices, but we'd be here all day if I were to show you all of them, so this will have to do."

Sir Thomas, with no other option, looked at the corpse of a woman who had been strapped down in a chair. Two circles were displayed in front of her eyes, a few inches away from the sockets. There was a cylinder an inch away from each ear. The woman had hundreds of pin-needles all throughout her body. "With God above me, what is that heinous machine?"

"I thought the name of the machine was self-explanatory, but I guess not," Francesca said as she threw her hands to either side of her head. "It destroys all of the senses, one at a time, making the person go insane. First, the circles in the front blind the victim using powerful lights that are so bright that they can even blind a person through their closed eyelids. That takes a lot of energy. Then, a thousand needles are stabbed into the body at specific points, taking away all feeling except for in the head. That way, the victim still feels pain when their tongue is cut off, and then when their ears blasted out," Francesca exclaimed gleefully with pride. "Ba-buh-bah-bum! After that, they mumble inaudibly, but I know what they're saying. They're asking me to end their miserable existence, and so I do just that. Well, just the one time, anyway. It turns out I don't like the machine, so that woman is the only one who got to use it. Take a look at her feet," Francesca commanded with a point toward the corpse.

Reluctantly, Sir Thomas looked at the feet of the woman, fearful of what he might see. He turned away in disgust when he saw what he had feared he would have seen: the woman's severed tongue, stained red with blood.

"Hard to stomach? I guess it would be for some people. I have no aversion to anything grotesque, but that makes total sense. After all, I *am* addicted to inflicting pain. I mean, could you *imagine* if I was squeamish or afraid of blood?" Francesca called manically, almost crying from sadistic joy. "How *ironic* would that be? The only thing that disturbed me was when Damon got rid of his mustache. He looked so manly and intimidating with it, but he got rid of it." She pushed a button on the remote, and the Sensory-Overloader disappeared back into the unholy depths of the floor. Francesca put the remote away. "See, I don't really care for the machines. They certainly test my building abilities and intelligence, but they aren't fun. It's not hands-on torturing, which is what I prefer. The machines are just for when I'm lazy but need to torture. Crazy, right? I also have plenty of prosthetic limbs that have been weaponized. Machine-gun-arms, buzzsaw arms, sword legs, and just a whole variety of fun weapons to use. Some are impractical, but they're all very interesting if I don't say so myself."

"Blimey!" Sir Thomas smiled. "Why didn't you just start off with that, Ms. Leach? I couldn't agree more on how interesting those prosthetic limbs are," Sir Thomas said excitedly, praising her with every note. "You're certainly an ace in the field of inventing. Any bloke could see that. In *fact*, you've impressed me so much that I think we should make a deal. You cut me free, and I'll help you sell them for billions of dollars to people without limbs. Sounds bloody fantastic, doesn't it?"

Francesca laughed heartily. "Please...*stop*! Hehehe. You'll turn me on too much. After all, I love it when my victims try to talk me into letting them go. It highlights the fear and hope they have, and those two things are vital for pain. People who are afraid will scream and plead, and people with hope can tolerate more pain. Either way, I have fun. Out of all of the reasons my victims have given me, your deal is certainly the most persuasive one so far, and I would've actually thought about it. We are a bit low on funds, but you're a special case, *Sir* Thomas. ***The Sinful Son*** is powerful, but he's held back by his morality and humanity. Born a monster and evil? That's not true at all. Damon was never made to deal with that, and he's always been a good person. Of course, I fixed that right away. I'm a bad influence, but Damon has a crippling need and weakness when it comes to women. He couldn't care less about sex or anything, but he emotionally needs to be bonded with a woman. I found him when he was weakest and took him in as a mother and a girlfriend, which he had been lacking. He's loyal and attached to me beyond death. However, I want you to understand that I helped him, and he is very grateful."

"Any bloke would know that's not true at all. Do you truly believe that you've helped him and that he's happy with the life he has?"

"I don't know what a 'bloke' is, but I don't appreciate your fancy talk or accusations. Damon has every reason to be grateful. I unleashed his true power. ***The Sinful Son*** would have stayed locked away if it wasn't for me, and living with that monstrous creature inside of him would have led to a painful existence and then his death. Besides that, I've given him food, technology, a place to stay, a purpose, and a way to get revenge without getting caught. I've even spent hours listening to all of his memories and stupid thoughts about life. Oh, and I tried erasing his childhood memories so he could live a happy and peaceful life. It's not my fault the experiment didn't work. He's always blamed me, but I didn't know it would go wrong. It was probably because of him that the experiment failed. He should be grateful it didn't kill him. He's mad that he forgot that his full name is Damon Willow-"

"Impossible! God spare me! So, he's related to Birch, after-"

"Don't interrupt me," Francesca snapped. "I'm ranting about how grateful Damon should be for all that I've done for him. He forgot his last name and a few useless memories, but he should be happy to have lost his last name since he hates his family so much. He *wanted* to forget. Not to mention that I'm pregnant after he fucked me, but he's not getting the child. No one is, because it'll die before it exits my body. Half of him and half of me? I couldn't think of a more terrifying thing to release into this world. Besides, he doesn't deserve to have a family."

"Who are you to decide that for him?"

"I know what's best for him!"

"Clearly not. Perhaps, he shouldn't be a father, but you don't get to decide that for him. Besides, if you truly loved him or wanted to help, you would have used his last name and the internet to find his brother who was sent away. If you knew Mr. Damon's last name, you could've reached out to Birch Willow, the famous gym owner, who is a living giant. There's a high possibility that they're related, and Birch would have gladly-"

"Would have what? Would have gladly taken Damon away from me after *I* saved him and helped him? I don't think so. Speaking of that giant, I saw the news. The attack on his gym in Charleston was different from what most weapons are capable of, and between that and what Damon reported, I know it was you. I want that gun you have. I *need* it. See, weapons and tools like that must work by destroying matter or atoms. For me, that's the ultimate ability because, with it, I could bring pain to a whole new level. I could bring pain to an *atomic* level." Francesca pulled out the Deconstructor Blade, and it began to glow sinisterly. "That man in the lab coat and the speedster are bound to come for you, but they won't know whether you're alive or not. So I'd start talking, you old bastard."

Sir Thomas looked at the threat of death directly in the eyes and smirked challengingly.

"What's so funny?"

"Start talking? Fear death?" Sir Thomas laughed. "I'm a holy knight of God and a servant of not only Him but also of **King Kronos**. I fear *nothing*," Sir Thomas stated boldly with pride, almost causing Francesca to step back a bit with anxiety from the commanding tone he spoke with. "You're the one who better start giving me information because I'm the one with secrets, and the unknown of my life is far more deadly than what you could ever hope to threaten me with." Between his time just spent with Damon and all of his years living with Kronos, besides all of the books he had read, Sir Thomas knew how to speak intimidatingly. "Would you believe me if I told you that the man in the lab coat planted a small atomic device inside of me that will devastate this entire building like that gym if I give it the command to do so? The moment you hurt me, I'll give it the command, and clamping my mouth shut won't help either. The machine is activated by recognizing the internal vibrations of a specific series, so I can just say the phrase without even opening my mouth. Granted, activating such a device would mean my death, but it would stop you and *The Sinful Son*, as well as end my suffering. Plus-" Sir Thomas stopped short as the Deconstructor Blade pierced his heart, it's atomic ability not activated.

"I'm fine with that," Francesca replied maliciously without any fear at all. Insanity was visible in her two different eyes. "I've never been afraid of death or what's beyond it, and that level of pain would be unparalleled when it comes to satisfaction." She pushed the knife deeper into her victim's chest. "How does it feel? The pain? The fact that your own knife is killing you? To top it all off, I'm not even using the atomic blade or whatever because that wouldn't be as much fun as this is." Her soft lips smiled wickedly with joy, but her eyes were cold and emotionless. "*Die*, old man," Francesca stated in a condemning whisper. "We'll go out together. Damon, me, and you- it all ends here."

Sir Thomas' whole body shook and trembled, his eyes bulging and his mouth spasming, as he was utterly shocked at the sudden attack and the failure of his bluff. He had doubted Francesca's willingness to die for her addiction. Staring down at the knife in his chest, there was no blood at all, but he still could not believe that it was real. He groaned in pain, but he would not give Francesca the satisfaction of hearing his screams or shocked cries of hopelessness. He did not have to force his mouth shut, however, as he barely had enough energy left to verbally reply. He felt his strength rapidly decline, and he could barely breathe. Yet, he was still conscious, and he managed to smile, his insides humming with a final chuckle.

"Have you gone delusional, old man? What could you possibly be laughing at as you die? Is the satisfaction of knowing that this building and I are going down with you all you need?"

There was another small chuckle from the dying man. "There isn't an atomic device," Sir Thomas spat out, "but there *is* him! Cheerio, bitch!" As upset as he was to not be able to finish the journey for a cure, see what kind of hero Timothy ended up, and what Kronos would ultimately do for the world, Sir Thomas died satisfied with his life as **The Sinful Son** and a storm of black smoke came rushing into the room like an unstoppable tsunami wave.

Kronos and Timothy arrived at the island shortly after they had patched themselves up and restocked. It had been tense between them at first, but they quickly got over their personal emotions. A simple aim of the D.O.O.M. Shooter at a fisherman had been enough to hijack a boat, and they had quickly sped over to the coordinates they were tracking. Since the technology Francesca had created hid the island, Kronos assumed the base was underwater when he did not see land. This had resulted in them passing through the barrier and crashing, but Kronos had slowed the boat down in time to land on the shoreline softly enough that they were not injured or killed.

Now, the two men, cautious and ready to kill, slowly made their way through the beautiful vegetation of the island. When the building was in sight, they crouched behind a bush.

Pulling out binoculars, Timothy put them to his face before scanning the building with them. He squinted through his steampunk goggles, having cleaned them off a bit, although they were still scratched on the left side. "Very odd. I don't see any perimeter defenses or any guards. The place seems completely abandoned. It looks like it hasn't been maintained at all, or if it's an old war base. We'll still have to be careful for traps and such, but I think it's just The Dark Depressor and his boss." He rubbed his scabbed cheek, which hurt from talking. Timothy examined the building some more. "I don't see a way in or any doors or windows from here. I should probably run around the whole island using my speed so that we-"

Timothy was cut off by the sound of collapsing bricks in the distance. He took his eyes out of the binoculars to see that Kronos was using the D.O.O.M Shooter. He was using the weapon to create a gaping hole in the wall of the building. He let his finger off of the trigger, and the yellow beam of electricity dissipated. Kronos gestured over to the hole he had just created in the side of the building. "Well, Timothy, there's your entrance. I make a way wherever I go, and it was insolent of them to think that having no obvious entrance would delay us. I'm not holding back anymore. We have to rescue him immediately, and it took us far too long to get here. Let's go!"

"Agreed. Time for the heroes to shine."

Kronos, prepared with his vast intellect, the Atomic Gauntlet, and the D.O.O.M Shooter, left the cover of the bush, running over to the building. Timothy, his powers not currently coursing through his body, followed behind Kronos, the broken but still deadly Whip-Watch ready for action as it swung in his hands.

Arriving at the hole in the building, the two men cautiously peeked their heads into the entrance. The hole led into an empty hallway, and they carefully stepped in. The bland lights overhead flickered slightly, and the hallway had several other passageways attached to it. Timothy followed behind Kronos, who stopped in the center of the hallway and glanced at all of the other ways they could go.

Timothy exhaled in frustration. "With all of these hallways, we'll never get to him in time! I wanted to save my powers, but I'll have to inject myself and speed-"

Kronos stopped Timothy with a raise of his hand. "That won't be necessary. You should save them, and you can, because I know where we have to go," Kronos stated as he pointed to black smoke lingering in the one hallway. "The Dark Depressor was just here a few minutes ago at most, and he'll most likely lead us to where they're keeping Thomas. Now, follow me but walk backward so they can't sneak up on us."

The two men followed the trail to the torture chamber, and after jumping down the staircase into the room, they stopped when they saw a woman sitting in a chair, her hands tied up behind her back. A brown paper bag was over her head with a note attached to it. Her body did not move at all, but she did not seem to be dead either.

"I don't like this," Timothy mumbled. "This could be a trap."

"Such a possibility is likely, but we cannot afford to waste time. I have always been a bit reckless, but that's because nothing and no one can stop me." Ignoring Timothy's warning, Kronos stormed over to the woman and ripped the paper from the bag. He quickly read the note, which had been written with what appeared to be human blood that was abnormally bright red. The paper seemed warm.

Scanning the room and checking behind him, Timothy swiftly made his way over to Kronos. "Well, what does it say? Who is this woman?"

"It would appear that The Dark Depressor is actually a man named Damon, and it's a long apology. He must write quickly, and even so, his handwriting is impeccable. According to him, he used his own blood as ink to further the sincerity of his words. Apparently, he and this woman had a fight. Her true identity is Mallory Leach, but she changed her name to Francesca, and she is also known as The Torturer. She chopped his left arm almost in half using Thomas' Deconstructor Blade. After fixing it with a prosthetic, he knocked her out but, ironically, lacked the anger and revenge needed to end her miserable life. He usually gets angry enough over the smallest agitations that he'd actually break laws and kill people over insignificant grudges, but it's a different case with her due to their history and relationship. She is addicted to inflicting pain and has been torturing people for decades. The kidnappings were for her, and she's the one who sent him to fight us. Anyway, he says that it's up to us how she is dealt with, and he's sorry, but…" Kronos crumbled the paper with his fingers as his grip tightened.

Timothy hesitated, fearing the bad news. "*But* what?"

The grip strength of Kronos' fingers began to tear holes into the crumbled paper. "It says that he was too late when it came to saving Thomas from Francesca's insanity and that if we seek the old man's body, look beyond her to the wall in front of us," Kronos muttered in heartbreak and rage. Without hesitation, Kronos looked up, glaring past Francesca, and, trembling with angry disbelief, he saw the body of Sir Thomas strung up and dead, the lifeless Deconstructor Blade in his chest. "Indeed, I see what he meant by that," Kronos stated coldly through clenched teeth, the vein on his forehead about to burst. The light reflecting off of the lenses of his high-tech sunglasses made the fiery lenses seem like they were burning. For a moment, he seemed to look like **The Sinful Son**. Viciously, Kronos bent the ends of each finger that resided in the cold metal of the Atomic Gauntlet, the metallic sounds cracking lethally in the silent chamber.

Noticing the deadly movement of Kronos' fingers through his watery eyes, Timothy began to panic. His heroic instincts sensed justified but rash villainy. He realized what was going to happen, and he lunged forward at his grieving friend. "Kronos, wait-"

It was too late. Not even a speedster was fast enough to stop him. Kronos, his metallic fingers outstretched like demon claws and glowing a sinister yellow with the unique current, dug into Francesca's chest with the sharp fingers of the Atomic Gauntlet before ripping out her heart. As he crushed the entire exposed organ in his metal hand, the current tore it apart atomically. When he opened the large hand of the gauntlet, nothing was left except for blood and a few red clumps that all fell to the ground. Then, before anything else could happen, Kronos violently ripped the bag off of Francesca's head. Although unconscious, her face still held a maniacal grin of insanity, her cheek and forehead scratched and dripping with blood. Kronos brought the D.O.O.M. Shooter to the middle of her face. He fired away, tracing a circle over and over her face, peeling it apart layer by layer from the center outward, as everything was destroyed, until her head was just a bloody mess of the cells the gun left behind. A piece of her spine stuck out through the top of her neck. It stained red as blood came spilling out from her neck like a volcano.

Covering his mouth with his hands at the grotesque sight and sobbing, Timothy cried. He cried for Sir Thomas. He cried for Francesca. He cried for Kronos. He cried over his failures as a hero. He had failed to defeat **The Sinful Son**. He had failed to save the innocent lives of those in need of his help. He had failed to protect and rescue Sir Thomas. He had failed to stop Kronos. Then, uncontrollable anger built up in Timothy, formed from the justice and morals that were barely hanging on inside of him. "Stop it," he demanded angrily through hot tears as he grabbed Kronos on the shoulder and turned him around so that the two men were facing each other. "*Stop it!* How could you do that? You monster! This could all be a trap, but worst of all, you could've just killed an innocent person without hesitation!"

The expression on Kronos' face was pure wrath and unstoppable power, backed by the immeasurable intelligence and experience needed for such inhuman power. Every feature, from his hair to his veins seemed severe. His eyes, despite being hidden behind technology, were ablaze and deadly. **"Incorrect!"** Kronos' voice boomed and echoed throughout the room with a different type of egotism. It was a firm resolution to actually use his power and get whatever he wanted. Every sound was cemented with the knowledge that he was absolutely correct. "*They* killed the innocent person. They killed my only friend. My only family member. My father. Did you see the look on her face? The Dark Depressor was telling the truth. Besides, there's no possibility of some woman being on this island that isn't related to the kidnappings," Kronos stated as he shifted his shoulder back, removing Timothy's hand from his shoulder without having to grab him.

"You don't know that! You may know a lot, but this isn't something that comes from studying or self-education. There's no proof of anything in that letter being true, and he could have easily grabbed her on his way over here as a decoy! You're going to believe The Dark Depressor over *me*? You're *wrong*, Kronos. Killing her was not the right thing to do."

"**Incorrect!** *You* lost all say in what is right or wrong when you failed to be a hero! Your morals aren't as pure as we all thought, and you're more selfish than any of us would have guessed. Thomas is dead because of you! So are all of those police officers who were killed. You let your obsession with being a hero ruin your chances of being one. Do you honestly think that The Dark Depressor grabbed a woman as a decoy on his way over here and then made all of that up? Don't forget that *you* attacked him first! I'm not blaming everything on you, because I'm certainly one to blame as well. I've never trusted anyone, but I gave you a chance. I thought you were great and were going to be the best hero this world has ever seen, even if you were the first and only one. The problem is, I was trusting you with more than just myself, and that was a grave mistake. For all your talk, your actions are utterly pathetic. If you wanted to stop me from killing that rotten woman, you could have, but you didn't because you're not a hero. You want to believe that you tried, but you knew that she deserved to die."

With no response to the harsh ruth, Timothy stayed silent as he clenched his left hand into a fist, ashamed of himself. His body internally shook with power and speed building up inside of him.

"It wasn't my intention to be cruel, but you must know the truth if you truly wish to grow and continue to try and be a hero. The path of redemption is different for everyone, but most people *are* able to walk down it if they want or need to. I, on the other hand, don't care about what fate awaits me or what I've done. I'm not saying that you can just look at a person and know whether or not they might be evil, but that woman was obviously corrupted if she was here, and she was supposedly the boss of The Dark Depressor, making her a villain far worse than he is or was. So, hate me for killing her if you want or have to, but I accept what I did. In fact, I'm glad that Thomas can now rest more easily. He believed in Heaven, and I never have, but for his sake, I hope there is one and that he's being warmly accepted there as we speak," Kronos said as he walked over to where Sir Thomas was strung up and dead. Carefully, but without hesitation, Kronos pulled the Deconstructor Blade out of his caretaker's chest. "Now, put your feelings away, Timothy. I need you to help me move him away from this accursed building." Using the knife, Kronos then cut the four ropes one at a time so that Sir Thomas would not fall forward, gently placing Sir Thomas on the floor.

Still silent, growing more unstable by the minute, Timothy hesitated a moment, still shaking internally. He wanted to rush over like a speeding train and smash his fist into Kronos' face, sending him into the wall behind him. He knew he could run at superhuman speeds even without his powers fully activated, and just running in a straight line would have little consequences. Yet, his body would not move. It was not because he was incapable of harming a friend, but his body felt that it would be destroyed if it tried to do what Timothy desired of it. He felt like he would lose in a fight against Kronos, especially since he was still healing. So, quickly walking, faster than the average jogging speed, Timothy walked over to Sir Thomas and grabbed his body by his fancy shoes. Lifting up the corpse, which was not yet cold, he and Kronos silently carried the body away without stopping until they reached the wrecked boat.

Kronos towered over the limp body on the sand. "Thomas was a good man and a gentleman, and the only bad he ever did was for me or because of me. His humor wasn't the best, but his cooking skills were remarkable. As we all know, he was a religious man, and the only one between him and I, so I know of no prayers or anything. I have no farewell to say except for the thoughts I hold in my mind." Kronos wiped a single tear, which had managed to slip through the microscopic gp between his skin and the sunglasses, away from his face. "Timothy, I ask that you pray for him, over him, or whatever it is that a proper death should have included besides my attempt at a speech. I'll just listen. I'm sure it's what he would want."

Timothy nodded his head. "Lord God, we come to you in the name of Jesus Christ on a day of tragedy. Today, many souls are moving on beyond life and death to a new eternal life. While we pray for all of those souls, we'd like to honor and pray for Sir Thomas, who is among those souls today. We pray that he is warmly received into Heaven, that he is blessed, and that we are comforted as we mourn. Amen."

"Correct, and agreed." Kronos looked at the screen that was built into the Atomic Gauntlet. *So, it's happening already. Looks like The Torturer has been spared of the future. At least she's lucky. It appears that two of our friends will be there when it happens, but I guess that was inevitable. We're all going to end up together, just like it wants us to be, and there's nothing I can do to stop it. Ironic, I suppose. The whole point of this journey was to prevent the future that I feared was approaching, and it's actually what has brought us all together. Did they plan for my plans to work for their plans? Have I been tricked? Have I been outmatched in a battle of strategic genius? So much for facing the future alone and sacrificing myself. At this rate, we'll all die together, or we'll barely manage to win. I could never imagine us overcoming such a threat, though. It's impossible.* Kronos dismissed the notifications on the screen with a grunt.

"What is it, Kronos? News report?"

"It's nothing. I've just been informed that the end of our journey together is almost near. A few of my security drones that were out on private investigations just informed me that two unidentified aircraft are on a route toward England. Just a short while ago, one of them departed from Cape Cod, Massachusetts, and it's a type of military cargo jet that seems to be flying hazardously as if the pilot is untrained. It just so happens that Cape Cod is where I was looking for

The Immortalizer. The other aircraft is a large plane that surpasses the size generally used by the military, and it departed from Charleston, West Virginia, a few moments after the one from Cape Cod departed. It's large enough for a giant to fit in. Given all of those facts, there's no doubt about it: The Immortalizer and The Ruthless Root are both heading for R.O.M.A.B.A. Industries in an attempt to get answers. The speed of both vehicles is faster than legally permitted, and at this rate, accounting for the time change between here and there, they'll be arriving just before sunset in England. We have to go there."

"How? You crashed our boat, and even if you could fix it, we still have the problem of getting a flight to England. It's *possible*, but the timing probably wouldn't align for us to get there fast enough, and that's not accounting for delays and cancellations."

"That's why you're going to search the island. Save your powers for the fight, but I want you to go over and check behind that building. It's most likely that those maniacs have an aircraft of their own here in order to go to and from the island. We know they have a boat, but that's not their only method of transportation. It wouldn't be logical. Yell if you need backup, as Damon is most likely somewhere on the island, but he seems to be out of the picture now."

"Don't get your hopes up, but I'll check," Timothy stated before jogging off toward the building at a superhuman speed that he could handle without a heightened nervous system, the particle suit leaving a trail behind him.

As soon as Timothy was gone, and Kronos was sure that he was truly gone, Kronos moved the clothes on Sir Thomas so that he could properly study and inspect the wound in his chest. He reached into his lab coat and slightly smirked. The small sandpipers gathered around the scientist and his fallen caretaker.

Less than a few minutes later, Timothy returned from his mission. He saw that Sir Thomas was now buried under a slight hill of soft sand, assuming that Kronos had used the Atomic Gauntlet to scoop large handfuls of the grains at a time. "There were two experimental jets of some kind, but one of them wasn't finished yet. That limits our option to just the one, which could be a trap, but it's our only choice. I don't actually know anything about flying or vehicles, but they look like they can go really fast. In fact, we should arrive in England shortly after the other two do."

"Correct. Oh, and there's one more thing, Timothy. I'm sorry for everything that's happened. Before we go, I'm going to give this to you, because I'm sure Thomas would have wanted you to have this," Kronos said earnestly as he handed Timothy the Deconstructor Blade. "His light has perished, but the current of his blade still shines.

"Thank you," Timothy said in a shaky voice as he gripped the handle of the sharp knife tightly with regret and guilt, but also a new determination to redeem himself and do good. "I think it's about time I finally visited R.O.M.A.B.A. Industries."

After secretly watching Timothy and Kronos fly away at insane speeds toward England in the one experimental jet, Damon returned to the dark hallways of the base.

"What... what happened?" Searching the darkness of the hallway, Damon spotted the source of the voice. It was Lilith, peeking her head out of her room and looking down the hallway at him. "I know this place isn't the most peaceful, but it's been really noisy. It sounded like fighting, and I think I just heard a big plane outside."

"Please return to your room, Lilith," Damon commanded, his voice still filtered into an even more monstrous one than it naturally was. ***"I don't have time to explain it all to you right now. There's no doubt that you'll have several questions that will interrupt my explanation, which is already going to be a long story. I have a phone call to go make that is critical to the future. I shall talk to you about it later, understood? I'll have to go soon, but I'll explain why and where before I go."***

Lilith nodded her head and then went back into her room, locking the door.

Traveling like a black tempest, Damon hurried through the darkness to his room and then to a cellphone he had hidden under the bed. He did not use technology or electronics often, but he had experience with such devices. Quickly, he called a single number on the phone. The person on the other end answered, and Damon talked to them for quite a while before hanging up.

The important phone call taken care of, Damon headed toward the rage-room he and Francesca had created together, anger building up inside of him exponentially with each second that passed. The memories and words of the past two days played in his head moment-for-moment as he relived all that had just happened, his mind trying to gather his thoughts and emotions and organize them.

Right outside of the room, Damon exited his unholy garments, breaking free from the vantablack cloak and advanced exosuit. They stood ominously like a statue against the wall in the dark hallway, and the abandoned garments seemed to be a living monster all on their own. Pulling his black shirt off, Damon was dressed in nothing but black pants, socks, and the metal boots that were detachable from the suit. His heart was pounding at unsurvivable speeds, hot sweat formed and evaporated on his skin, his head throbbed, his blood heated up, his teeth clenched together like a set-off bear trap, and his whole body was constantly tensing and relaxing, his muscles ready to immediately kill anything. He gave off a physical aura of extreme heat, and he gave off a psychological and emotional aura of death and punishing destruction. Damon burst into the room uninvitedly, and he was maliciously content to see that it had been restocked and cleaned since the last time he had used it.

Bursting into the rage-room with a powerful slam of the door against the inside wall as he opened it violently, shaking the entire building, Damon immediately got to work, screaming monstrously and releasing everything inside of him physically through martial arts, violence, and pure destruction. Occasionally, Damon would use melee weapons in the rage-room to truly get destructive, but when his emotions were reaching high levels of uncontrollable wrath, he just smashed and attacked everything with his own hands and feet, which he had turned into indestructible weapons through years of brutal training. The freedom of not relying on weapons and tools allowed him to destroy more viciously. The only difference now was that he had a prosthetic limb for his left arm, but it was highly advanced, designed to kill, and its owner would never even know that they lost a limb.

"They are SICKENING with their constant bickering and littering of the world of emotion and loyalty. Not a MOMENT of relaxation or peace! They won't leave ANYTHING for me. NOTHING. I can't have anything at all except having my entire mind collapse and FALL!" Damon punched right through the glass screen of an old fashioned television. His hand and bones, hardened by years of training and burning with unnatural heat created by revenge and rage, were unscathed as he ripped his deadly fist out of the hard machine, sending glass flying and shattering. He spun around like a tornado before charging at the wall. *"DIE a thousand times over in the most torturous ways, you ungrateful BEASTS. It's not fair, not fair, not fair, not fair,"* Damon's voice grew louder and more violent with each word as he began to relentlessly punch the wall, cracking it with each hit as he let all of his rage loose, *"not fair, not fair, not fair, not fair, not fair, not fair, NOT FAIR!"* He stopped as his left fist collided powerfully and formed a large and deep crater in the reinforced walls, which had been specifically designed to contain his wrath. Since his emotions and body were so unstable, and since his power had no limits and constantly changed, Francesca had made the walls based on mere estimates. *"Your walls fail me just as much as you did, MALLORY! How PATHETIC!"*

Damon spun around even more violently than before, and he sent a sturdy table flying with a monstrous kick. *"I WASTED MY LIFE on you and your false promises! Curse you, MALLORY!"* He ran toward where he had kicked the table, and bringing his hands together and then down, he smashed the table into two pieces. *"Your death has set THE SINFUL SON completely FREE, and now there is nothing left of ME! Longing after a woman who did not love me was arrogant and unfortunate. I will never get those years back, nor shall my heart ever be complete. What is wrong with ME? What is wrong with YOU? You ruined everything? I wanted to DIE, but even YOU couldn't let me have ANYTHING THAT I WANTED! It's not fair! NOTHING IS FOR ME! EVERYTHING IS FOR EVERYONE ELSE! WHY IS MY WORLD LIKE THIS? Die, die, die, die, die, die, die, die, die DIE,"* Damon chanted monstrously as he repeatedly smashed the broken table fragments with his hands.

Hundreds of words and thoughts ran through his fractured mind and broken heart, but Damon could not connect them together to say anything philosophical or perfect for winning an argument. There was no rhyming. There was no logic or sense. All he could do was bellow the most powerful ideas echoing in his rage-filled mind as he destroyed. Everything else would remain trapped, but the strong ones broke free.

Grabbing the largest fragment left of the table, Damon violently spun around in a circle several times. *"They aren't even worthy of drinking my acidic piss!"* Releasing his grip on the piece, Damon sent the fragment flying across the room and into a wall. The collision thundered, and the piece broke into even smaller fragments. *"THE SINFUL SON has taken over because, without him, I am nothing but a ragdoll for all of you to kick around. HE won't allow you to do that ANYMORE! Speedsters? Scientists? Torturers? I DON'T WANT ANY PART OF THAT. The days long past aren't what I yearn for, nor the days to come. I HATE ALL of you. Every last one of you shall be KILLED BY MY OWN HANDS for the sake of Damon! A man plagued and cursed with too much humanity rejects it because none of you allow true human beings to live or prosper! You all lack humanity. Society is false!"*

Damon went on an unstoppable rampage, destroying everything in the room, which was filled with books, random electronics from all ages, tables, chairs, glass, stone, metal, and anything and everything that could be used as a substitute for human beings. That was why Damon had created the room because when his rage truly surfaced, it had to be released. There were no emotions or morals that could shove such hatred back into him. It would destroy everyone and everything in sight, and in order to prevent himself from creating such an unholy catastrophe, Damon and Francesca had built the room as an alternate world. The room of miscellaneous junk was a world where he could release all of his power and negative emotions without human casualties. Over the years, Damon began to care less and less about not hurting people, his tongue had almost ripped apart as he held back foul language, his arms had quaked as he restrained his own muscles, and his hormones and lust had almost consumed him, but he prevented all of that from happening, pushing himself beyond the emotional limits of most people. His god-like self-control was inspirational and admirable, and it was a heavy burden and a skill that was not natural or easy to maintain. He had still kept his humanity, and he had intended to always keep it. Otherwise, he knew that all would be doomed, including himself, in the end.

Now, however, Damon did not know and could not think of a single reason why *The Sinful Son* should be suppressed. There seemed to be no reason why *The Sinful Son* should not kill all or why he should have to help others. Even Lilith had faded from his mind. Damon could think of only one person who needed to be saved, and that was himself. All purpose in his life was gone. All that remained was the darkness he had always lurked in after being forced into it by others. Now, everything he had ever believed or known seemed to be meaningless and worth nothing. Francesca was gone. His family was long gone. His enemies were long gone. The past was a nightmare. The present was just as horrific. The future was undoubtedly empty. Nothing remained for him.

Yet, Damon did not even have himself left. The unholy truth was that the thing he was enraged at the most and hated more than anything was himself. He hated ***Damon,*** and he hated ***The Sinful Son.*** Both of them were to blame. He could not deny the faults of others, but in the end, he realized that everything was, in a way, his own fault. That was the unholy truth behind his attempted suicides and even his successful one, and it was an unholy truth that grew darker and more true with each passing day. His suicides were not because he could no longer tolerate the world, his greatest enemy, but because he could no longer bear his true worst enemy, himself, and the internal battles he fought daily. He hated even himself. With that, he truly despised everything in all existence.

Shooting out volcanic air from his nostrils in hurricane-like exhales, Damon slowly thudded toward the door. His walk was slow but exerted unstoppable power and rage, and his overwhelming dark aura only grew stronger. It had been only a short session of free-rage, and the emotional trauma of the past two days would last him several lifetimes. He exited the rage-room, each step a menacing earthquake, his entire body tense and ominous enough that just touching it would cause death. The air around him attempted to escape the aura of destruction, but his lethal lungs pulled in the fleeing victims with powerful breaths of hatred and rage and then expelled them from his body like a destructive sandstorm on the surface of a blazing sun. His demonic eyes were sore from holding back tsunami-tears behind the condemning orbs in the dark sockets, but he refused to cry. His hot anger evaporated the salty water. The natural disaster contained in a single biological being stepped into the dark hallway as a hollow vessel that knew what it had to do. Prepared for ***The Sinful Son*** to use it at the cost of death, Damon clothed himself in the unholy garments one final time before he viciously traveled like a dark storm toward the exit of the base as he headed for the remaining experimental aircraft.

CHAPTER 5

A DOCTOR'S DIAGNOSIS

(Somewhere in England. Later That Same Day: April 18, 2022.)

Taking a long sip of his drink, Abraham put his phone away with a smile before walking into the room where Birch Willow was waiting with a stern expression on his face. "Why the glum expression, Mr. Willow? We're going to be right above R.O.M.A.B.A. Industries' largest building in a few minutes, so make sure you're mentally ready for your mission. That's their public store, but it's been closed down while they've been gone. I suggest you pay it a visit."

Birch turned toward Abraham gruffly. "So what exactly is the plan for once I get there? You just drop me off, and then I wreak havoc and chaos 'cross the place 'til they show up? I'm sure they've got the best security in the world, so I'll be detected, but you said that they were in Florida this morning. Are ya sure they'll be here?" Birch cracked his giant knuckles, the sound far louder than what a normal human could hope to make.

"I'm afraid you're mistaken, Mr. Willow." Abraham chuckled as he took another sip from his drink. "We're not dropping you off. On the ground, that is. Landing our aircraft would be possible, but the attention it would draw would be very hard to deal with. There's a reason we're so high in the sky and partially cloaked. You'll be parachuting down, but don't worry, we have a parachute that'll be able to support your weight along with your gear. Between your natural mass and the heavy suit, it's a lot of weight, but our material will be able to handle it. They *are* on their way here, and while they won't be here as soon as you land, they'll be here soon enough. The jet they're on is an experimental one, and whoever is flying is skilled and reckless. We have some of the best technology in the world, but the size of this behemoth limits how fast it can go."

"Hmph. So, that monster in Florida was uh genius as well? That's uh bit frightenin' tuh think. Now, you said that you want Kronos fuh interrogation purposes and such. So, if it gets too dangerous, should I retreat instead of killin' 'im?"

"I'm sure your big heart will know what to do when the time comes. Hopefully, he'll just surrender at the sight of you, but I'm sure that he won't give up that easily." Abraham began to walk out of the room and back into the laboratory area of the plane. "Follow me, Mr. Willow. It's just about time. I can feel us slowing down."

Birch followed Abraham through the laboratory area, past the vehicles and crates, and into the cargo bay. Going over to the suits, Birch put on the armor that matched the colors and design of a willow tree. He then strapped on the large backpack containing the parachute as the back of the plane opened up.

"Damn! I'm impressed, Mr. Willow. You look amazingly terrifying, and I believe you'll do great out there. Wow! It's been an honor, and I'm looking forward to the results of this mission. I know you don't like or trust me, nor do you like or trust The Organization. Despite our differences, however, I really like you, Mr. Willow. You're a good man and a remarkable creation of science. However, as Abraham gave up Issac, or at least was going to, I must say goodbye for now. Hopefully, I'll see you soon. Make sure you kick ass out there. Take care, big fella," Abraham said as he saluted Birch heartedly.

Birch simply nodded his head before he stomped over to the open area, his footsteps even heavier than they naturally were. He truly seemed like an unstoppable giant now. As the wind whipped viciously, growing calmer as the plane slowed down, Birch looked through the clouds at the ground below. It was approaching sunset, and the rolling fields and hills were illuminated by a weakening orange light of warmth. Birch had never been scared of heights, but the altitude they were at was frightening, and a man as large of himself had never thought about skydiving. Without thinking about it anymore, he jumped out of the plane, falling toward the ground like a meteorite.

Ripping through the air like a rocket, Birch was on a course to land directly in front of the lifeless store like a nuclear warhead. At the right time, he pulled the parachute, soaring backward before slowly falling toward the ground, a bit faster than he expected. He landed with a heavy thud, smashing the soft ground and breaking it apart.

Birch tore the backpack off of him before throwing it away from himself. He looked up at the massive building that stood before him. The helmet had been designed to protect Birch's face while still allowing him to see, though his vision was a bit restricted. The inside of the building was cold and dark, but the large letters of a white glowing sign read "R.O.M.A.B.A. INDUSTRIES" across the top front of the store. It was locked down with metal gates across the doors and large front windows, but Birch could tell that everything inside was definitely valuable. Multiple posters were displayed in the front windows that apologized to customers for the inconvenient closure, but that the store would soon be open again, and that their online store has everything plus almost instantaneous shipping.

As he inspected the front of the building, Birch internally shook with a feeling of being watched. He spotted cameras that were on either side of the front of the building, and he knew that there were most likely hidden cameras as well, but the feeling was stronger than that. Hearing what sounded like slight buzzing in the distance, Birch glanced around for what he suspected to be a security drone. He was unable to find it. The artificial buzzing disappeared, and it was dead quiet. There were no animals nearby, including birds and bugs, which made Birch all the more cautious and spooked. There was nothing but flat fields of brown and green for acres around the store with a few trees, and beyond those were just rolling hills. The store was practically in the middle of nowhere, and it stood like the castle-center of an empire. A finely paved path led to the parking lot on the right side of the building, but the road seemed to stretch infinitely away from the store.

Deciding to check out the entire perimeter of the store, Birch headed left, turning around the corner of the large building. Just a few thudding steps later, he stopped short when he saw a figure in the distance. It was an ominous man walking alongside the building and inspecting it just as Birch was. The man was in a tattered war uniform and was wearing a black mask that was unlike any kind Birch had seen. Without hesitation, Birch charged at the man with the force of a rhino. He launched through the air with a raised fist, his full beastly power behind the dangerous skull-breaker.

The man, however, had been instantly alerted by Birch's thudding footsteps, mistaking the shaking of the ground for a small earthquake below him. Seeing the attack bound to pulverize him, he caught the giant fist with his hands, stopping the lethal punch just a few inches away from his face. The ground below him cracked for six feet around him as he fell to one knee. His arms shook ferociously and began to bend backward as he struggled against the powerful force being brought down on him.

Birch pulled his fist back. "No regular human could ever hope tuh hold back such uh force as that. Hmph. Uh normal person would've been killed by that attack, their whole skull broken by uh single blow. The strength o' muh mighty attack seemed tuh go right through ya into the ground. I knew Kronos wasn't cheap when it came tuh protectin' his business, but uh security guard like you is uh bit shocking tuh discover."

"Wait, you know Kronos?"

"Of course, I know 'im! He came and destroyed everything I ever worked for in life, and 'e endangered the lives of innocent civilians. All o' it was vaporized into nothin' but atomic dust and such. You already took muh gym, but you won't be takin' me or anyone else!"

"I'm-"

Without hesitation, Birch burst forward and grabbed the man by his ankles before whipping him around and fatally slamming him into the ground several times like he was playing Whack-A-Mole, the ground breaking apart wherever he smashed the man. "I'm sorry tuh do this, but it ain't anything against you personally. For the safety of the future, I can't allow anyone from Kronos' heinous company live tuh endanger us all with crazy technology," Birch declared as he threw the man away from himself.

The man rolled over and slowly stood up. He brushed the dirt off of his tattered uniform while shaking his head in disbelief "This uniform managed to survive World War I without damage, but today has destroyed it. That's unbelievable. Then again, today is the day I'm finally destroyed, so I guess that makes sense." The man stretched his back and limbs before he cracked his neck. "Although, I wasn't expecting this at all. That was a brutal beating, and probably the worst I've ever suffered physically. You even managed to make me think I might end up paralyzed or dead." The man's dark gaze turned over to Birch like a laser. "I think it was rude of you to attack me without warning or reason, but I'll let it slide since there's been a misunderstanding. I don't work for Kronos or his company. I don't even know who he is. As far as I know, we're here for the same reasons. It took me a few seconds to recognize you, but you're Birch Willow, aren't you?"

"Guess I'm more famous than I thought," Birch grumbled loudly as he cautiously took a step forward, his muscles tensed and ready. "Then again, I *am* uh man with uh recognizable and unique build, so I guess it ain't hard tuh know it's me. Hmm. I'm willin' tuh talk things out, as I s'ppose it *was* unfair o' me tuh attack ya like that. I'm guessin' that you're one of the others Kronos was yappin' about, right? He mentioned an immortal man, and you still aren't dead or injured from muh attacks, so I'm guessin' you're him?"

"I guess *I'm* more famous than I thought as well. Word of individuals with powers sure spreads like wildfire when you have a man teleporting around telling everyone. After remaining unknown to the world for so long, I'm a bit bummed out that my streak of secrecy is over, but there's nothing I can do about that." The man walked over to Birch before putting his right hand out. "John Leach at your service. Otherwise known as The Immortal Man or Cape Cod Crusader."

"That last name is an interestin' one, tuh say the least." Birch accepted the outstretched hand and shook it as best as he could, his powerful hand much larger than John's invulnerable one was. "That's uh strong grip ya got. Birch Willow. Otherwise known as Charleston Crusher. When I was told about ya, I didn't believe you actually existed." Birch looked at the crater in the ground from where John had struggled against the first punch, and then at all of the spots where the ground had been hit with John's body. "I s'ppose anything is possible nowadays, though. I've seen some crazy things these past few days, and uh maniac with uh gun did destroy muh entire gym. You're much stronguh than uh regular person, and you seem more invulnerable than immortal. After all, you aren't healin' or nothing. I don't understand it, but you seem tuh have superhuman powers besides being immortal, as immortality doesn't give ya powers."

"The two *are* connected, though. However, I'm not immortal by magic but by science. Just to make that clear if it wasn't. It's hard to tell, but I'm actually wearing a suit over my skin. It's transparent and thin, but it's also almost indestructible. To summarize it up as simply as I can, the suit's atomic structure allows forces and energy to flow through it, just as you saw when you tried to punch me. Naturally, external forces that hit me are directed down my legs, to my feet, and then into the ground. However, if I stick my arms out, then it flows down them if the force is chest level or higher. The suit protects me externally from cuts, bullets, trauma to my insides, and from the sun, while this mask protects me internally by regulating my diet and the air I breathe. It's essentially a system that is made up of two separate parts that form the perfect creation when combined. As for my strength, well, I'm the healthiest human alive and have been for over a hundred years, so I perform at higher levels than normal humans when it comes to physical stuff. Of course, I'm no match for your superhuman strength."

"Forget about all o' that science crap! You're over uh hundred years old? You look like you're only thirty or forty!"

John smirked behind the mask. "That's how immortality works, big guy." He laughed a bit. "Thirty or forty? I'm glad there's a ten-year gap between the two ages I look like. That's certainly interesting to know. Still, those are nice numbers given the fact that I just turned one hundred and twenty-two years old." He laughed a bit. "You're shocked, aren't you? I can't believe it myself. All of my memories seem so long and so short at the same time. Either way, I look pretty good, don't I?"

"For someone that old, you don't look too shabby. Anyway, I'm here fuh revenge, as you probably know. Kronos is on his way, but he's not alone, s'pposedly. Besides that, I need tuh stop 'im before he bothers anyone else. We may be individuals with powers that intrigue others, but that doesn't give anyone the right tuh interfere with our lives. It ain't right, and he's hurtin' people. I can't stand by and watch. I would've stopped him if I had known he was doin' this, but I didn't, and it just so happens that I was his first target that he was actually able tuh meet. So, let me ask ya, John: why are you here?"

John's dark gaze shifted to a serious one of determination, and a breath rose in his chest before leaving through the mask. "Unfortunately, I'm not here for noble reasons or revenge. I've lived a long time with a darkness inside of me, trapped inside of this suit and behind the mask while I mentally rot from the inside out. I have no purpose in life or any reason to live. Corrupted by my depression and suicidal thoughts, I've tried to end my life several times, but that's almost impossible to do when you're immortal and invulnerable. At least, that's what I had believed until I met Kronos. Well, I never met him, but he came snooping around my local area looking for me. An acquaintance of mine told me that Kronos teleported away, and then I heard about the damage done to your gym. His creation is what I need to get this suit and mask off of me so that I can die."

Birch was somberly shocked. He looked at the mysterious man before him, wondering what he had lived through during his long years of immortality. "Are ya sure about that? I can't imagine what immortality has done tuh ya emotionally, so I can't tell ya what tuh do, but there's no turnin' back once it's done. No matter what lies beyond death, this life is basicallu the only one we get, if that makes sense. It seems tuh me that you have the most powerful creation out o' any of us individuals, and you should take advantage of it."

"I'm aware of that and was told by a girl who longs for me to come home how valuable life is and how stupid suicide is, but death has been my only goal in life. People spend their entire lives trying to achieve one goal sometimes, and I guess I'm one of those people. Now, I can finally accomplish the one task I've ever had in life. I can *die*. So, trust me, I'm sure about this. It's not even about what I've lived through or what I *could* do. My body is the healthiest one to exist, but it shut down a long time ago, along with my mind and heart. I'm sure you think you can convince me to live, but we're out of time to talk." John pointed past Birch. "It's time for me to steal one final breakthrough. I stole this suit and mask, and now I shall steal the only weapon capable of destroying them. A thief? Not at all," John stated with a shake of his head. "Just a foolish man, who was blessed with something that I am not capable of handling or using properly." John took a powerful step of sorrowful resolve forward, him and Birch now next to each other but facing opposite directions.

Turning around to see what John had been pointing at, Birch already knew in his heart what was there, or rather, *who* was there.

Walking toward Birch and John, the sun just about to begin setting behind the approaching figures, were two silhouettes. The figure on the left was swinging around a spiked sphere on a chain, and their whole body moved like a powerhouse of speed and energy. To that figure's left, a more terrifying silhouette approached with sinister steps, the outline of a lab coat flowing in the slight wind ominously, the lethal shape of a gauntlet, and the outline of an experimental gun.

There was silence.

None of the four men spoke.

The two teams of two men began to walk toward each other.

Then, in an instant, all four men were charging at each other, ready to fight and die if they had to. One ran forward for revenge and peace. One ran forward for selfishness and death. One ran forward for redemption and heroics. One ran forward just because they could. Both teams of men ran toward each other across the brown and green fields, ready to end the chaotic journey they had all been on.

Just as the men were within reach of each other and about to fight, they heard two helicopters in the sky. Turning away from each other, they were about to search the sky when a giant metal ring with a circumference that pressed them all together fell to the ground, destroying the dirt and grasses, and trapping the four men. Each of their backs were pressed against another's as they each faced a different way. Squirming, confused, and angered, they looked to the sky to see that two helicopters had dropped the trapping ring before quickly flying away. A multitude of vehicles sped onto the scene, and soon all four men were surrounded by a seemingly endless amount of people of all genders and races.

Birch noticed one crucial thing about these attackers that none of the other men caught on to. He heard the words of Abraham echo in his head but with a different meaning. The people surrounding them were all dressed in the same cliche fashion: a black business suit with black shades. All of them were agents of The Organization.

"It's uh trap!" Birch yelled this as he struggled against the metal ring trapping the four men, which even he, with all of his strength unleashed, could not move.

"Kronos, you son of a bitch! I came here to die, but this is just annoying and public shaming," John hissed out.

"Incorrect, The Immortalizer. Why would I trap Timothy and I along with you and Birch? That doesn't make sense. Your many decades of life must have rotted your brain all the way through to say something so stupid," Kronos retorted. He shook his head in frustration, seeing that his gauntlet and gun were pressed against him, making it impossible for him to use against the metal.

"John, this isn't Kronos," Birch stated. "As much of an asshole as he is, I have tuh agree with 'im. Right now, we're stuck in uh trap made by a group known as The Organization."

"As I predicted," Kronos muttered. "I thought I was outsmarting their outsmarting, but that was actually them using my unfathomable genius to their own advantage."

"What are you talking about, Birch?" John asked.

"Go on, Mr. Willow," Abraham yelled as he approached the trapped men. "Tell them about what's going on here since you seem to know. This is like an early Easter gift, ain't it? Congratulations on an outstanding job, Mr. Willow. As for the rest of you people, allow me to introduce myself. I'm Abraham, the third highest-ranking member of a group that Mr. Willow knows as The Organization, though our true identity is something different."

Birch was pissed beyond belief, and he was not entirely surprised by what was going on. "You set me up? This was uh trap tuh get all of us at once? Impossible. How did ya know that John was going tuh be here too, or is he just uh bonus? I can't believe you would violate our rights like this."

"Mr. Willow, please don't take any of this personally. I *actually* like you, and I wish that we could've been friends, but I'm afraid that it's what *they* want, not what I want. This is beyond my control or power. Prepare and brace yourselves men, as you're about to meet the two leaders of everyone here."

Abraham turned aside as three more silhouettes walked towards the four men, the sun nearly about to set behind the approaching shadows that walked with absolute power. It almost looked like the three figures were walking out of the blazing sun itself. The shadows showed one man, one woman, and one small girl standing in between the two. They were all holding hands as they approached the captured men. They were only fully visible to Kronos and Timothy, who were facing their direction. Birch and John, on the other hand, were facing the other way at an angle, and they had to crane their necks to see most of Abraham and the divine silhouettes.

John's shattered heart, darkened by decades of depression and suffering, burst with absolute terror and hopelessness as his pale skin grew ghostly, and his dark eyes became lifeless blackholes. "N-n-n-no. It can't be," John uttered in a trembling whisper of grave fear as he saw the three figures approaching. They were drawing nearer with each second, and as soon as they were no longer silhouettes, John saw that the man and women were wearing masks that were identical to the one he had stolen and worn ever since. "It just can't, but… it *has* to be *them*. Those masks. The creators," John whispered like death's farewell kiss. "They're here. They're real." Panicking, John instantly began to struggle like a fish in a net to escape.

Seeing the man deemed immortal and invulnerable panic and freak out, the hearts of the other men could not help but drop. Timothy's whole body shook like a powerhouse of anxiety. Birch braced himself by tensing his massive muscles, and he controlled his breathing as he prepared for the worst. Even **King Kronos** shivered a little bit.

Once the man, woman, and little girl were no more than a few feet away from the group, Abraham went down to one knee and bowed. "It is with humbleness, pride, and honor, that I am able to present to you the success of our operation."

The man, a gruff but charming individual, who appeared to be in his late forties, raised his right hand in a gesture for Abraham to stop. "As I expected, Abraham. You've done an outstanding job, and the success of our operation so far reflects greatly on why you have such a high position in our company," the man complimented in a slight Western accent. "I respect humility when it is necessary or done out of respect and honor, but today, you can be a prideful man, Abraham. The future greatly appreciates what you've done here today for the greater good. You are dismissed from this operation, as I will handle everything from here. I'm actually feeling generous, so know that you shall be rewarded tenfold of what you were originally promised. I bless doubly for what you have suffered, as I know this cost you a lot of time that could have been spent with your family. I bid you adieu, Abraham." The man nodded his head, his brown hair staying perfectly in place, his green eyes unreadable.

The woman, who had wavy blonde hair halfway down her back and lovely brown eyes, squatted down and whispered to the little girl. After listening to the woman, the little girl nodded her head. Informed that Abraham was leaving and would be away on vacation soon, the little girl was told to say goodbye to him. She did as she was commanded, her hazel hair bouncing behind her as she skipped over to Abraham. Just a child and innocent, for the most part, lacking an understanding of what was going on, she had a sweet voice. "Goodbye, Uncle Abraham," she said as she hugged his leg. "I'm sad to know that you'll be gone for a while, and I'll miss you. Have fun, though!"

The little girl returned to her parents as Abraham walked away into the sunset. He took one look back at the four men, making eye contact with Birch. He nodded his head in what seemed like an apology. Turning around, he walked away, off into the sunset to get on with the rest of his life, and to enjoy a break from having worked so hard for the past few years. His work here was done.

The man, his presence overwhelming, did not move closer to the men, but when he spoke, it seemed as if he were whispering into their ears, despite the mask on his face. "Well, they do say that parting is such sweet sorrow, but you'll see him before tomorrow. In fact, he'll be back in just a few seconds. Therefore, given the inevitable interruption about to happen, I shall not introduce myself just yet." The man pointed behind him over his shoulder in perfect unison of a gunshot sounding in the distance.

Just as the man had stated, Abraham was swiftly approaching the group, running as quickly as he could out of the sunset. He was half limping and waving his arms. "Code Dark! Code Dark! Move your asses! I need backup!" Two agents ran over to help Abraham as a squadron of them ran over to see what was going on.

Timothy cackled and laughed uncontrollably, hope resonating in each note. "Oh, man! You guys are screwed now! How ironic!"

Looming in the distance on the top of a hill, the sunset at its most powerful blaze of unstoppable power behind him, **The Sinful Son** stood ominously towering over the group in the distance as if he were a demonically divine being, larger than ever. Black smoke began to stream out of either side of him, and the darkness began to block out the setting sun like a solar eclipse. He was a monstrous silhouette as he stormed forward, the soft ground crumbling apart with each powerful step as he charged forward, unstoppable and lethal.

Abraham pointed at the monster in the distance. "Agents, stop that maniac at all costs. Go! I want at least *fifty* of you there *now*!"

Without hesitation or questions, fifty agents bravely charged at the dark hurricane jumping out of the blazing sunset at them. Each agent pulled out a pistol, aimed at **The Sinful Son**, and fired several rounds.

"After I said you did a good job, you go and prove that you are still overwhelmed by fear," the man remarked to Abraham, who was being supported by a female agent. "You let getting shot overwhelm you, and so you failed to notice how you got shot. So, watch as fifty brave men and women die instantly because of your mistake." The man turned and pointed to the brutal scene. "May the mourning of their families haunt your mind for all eternity."

The half of his left arm that had been severed now replaced by an advanced machine gun prosthetic, **The Sinful Son** continued to stomp menacingly toward the four captured men. Supporting his weaponized limb with his right hand, Damon used the machine gun at full power, easily killing multiple agents at a time as he mowed through them, going from left to right as he murdered without hesitation. The agents, obedient to death, continued forward, shooting at him. The bullets, however, could not penetrate his cloak, as Sir Thomas had learned earlier that day. It seemed impossible, but *The Sinful Son* had just killed fifty people in less than a minute.

"You fools! He's bulletproof," Abraham yelled as he was carried over to one of the many vehicles parked at the scene. "A bunch of you will have to get close and overpower him by hand!" Abraham quickly got into the car, which sped away past the building behind the four men, and he did not look back.

Listening to the final command Abraham had given, twenty more agents joined the charging attack against *The Sinful Son*, whose sneering laughter echoed overpoweringly amongst the darkness of the black smoke that surrounded him, striking fear into the hearts of everyone there except for Kronos and the man. ***How insolent of you pathetic weaklings to think that I, The Sinful Son, can actually die. To think that mere bullets could pierce my skin and that by shooting me, you could win, is undoubtedly an unforgivable sin. None of you have suffered what I went through decades ago, and none of you could ever hope to imagine or know. Powered by uncontrollable anger, rage, hate, and wrath, I shall continue to use your corpses to form a path. I shall use your blood to fill a bath, and know that the smoke is more than just black.*** The machine gun ran out of bullets, and Damon switched the weaponized prosthetic with a high-tech arm that matched his body size but was far stronger than his demonic strength. ***I have always felt that guns are for the weak, and now you'll see that my unholy powers are about to peak!***

Rushing forward like a raging sandstorm across a desert that consumed everything in its path, *The Sinful Son* charged into the group of agents that had been running toward him and jumping over the many bodies of their fallen allies, which were covered with bullet holes, some of them still groaning and crying out in pain. Having been joined by reinforcements, about thirty agents total collided with the menacing creature that towered over all of them. The scene engulfed in black smoke and chemicals, the four men, as well as everyone else, could not see what was going on in the battle that was taking place just a few feet away from them. All they could see was the dark storm that was spitting out agents, both alive and dead, and all they could hear were screams, curses, and cries for help.

When the black smoke dissipated and spread out thin enough that the battle scene was visible, everyone only saw one thing in the center of a setting sun. ***The Sinful Son*** was standing on a literal pile of corpses, six feet high, that he had made, and his figure was blacker and more ominous than ever as he towered over everyone, despite the distance between them. The only person who seemed to match the height of the menacing figure was the man, who stood tall and erect, staring up into the blazing red eyes a few feet away from him on top of a pile of his agents. Damon's breathing was not scattered or heavy, but he was perfectly calm and unscathed. His unholy garments whipped through the air to his left from the increasing wind, and it was a cinematic-like scene of unholiness. All-consuming rage chained to him by grudges and formed from the constant monstrous memories of his unsurvivable life powered every cell of Damon's demonic being, and it was visible in every speck of black that coated his sinister silhouette. His artificial eyes almost perfectly matched the blazing sunset behind him.

"Holy crap! This guy is unstoppable," Timothy commented with a laugh, hopeful that ***The Sinful Son*** would save him and the other three men that were trapped, ending the villains who stood before him, still unidentified but undoubtedly powerful. "Guess you should call it a day, old man. Let us free now, and we might just let you get off easy."

The man turned around, his gaze like a wave of death. All of the cockiness and hope drained from Timothy, replaced by a fear that made his squished body tremble. "You should shut your mouth, young Timothy, as I don't care for you too much, and I already knew that Damon would be here. Unlike you, I knew that he was going to quickly repair the second experimental jet and then fly over here. The only reason he's still standing and free, unlike you four, is because I'm enjoying witnessing power that is almost equal to one-sixth of mine if it's even that high." The man narrowed his green eyes, and Timothy struggled to stay awake and alive. "We'll capture him soon enough, but his strength, determination, wrath, and power are all admirable and worthy of my respect. So, I shall allow him to survive for as long as he can." Turning around with a stern face of mysterious intelligence, the man signaled to an agent, who was sitting in a white electric car. "Will he stop the car using his own strength, or will he make the decision to jump onto the vehicle and crash through the windshield? Jumping is smarter, but he'll just resist it instead. That's my prediction, which is absolute."

Obeying the man's command, the vehicle quickly sped off toward the mound of corpses that *The Sinful Son* was standing on in an attempt to hit him. Forced to run over a few bodies of agents who had been thrown toward the group, the car sped toward its target. Jumping down like a meteorite and planting his feet firmly in the soft ground, burying them an inch, *The Sinful Son* braced himself. With a monstrous vocal outburst that echoed across the land, the sinister living-shadow caught the car with outstretched arms that then bent to ninety-degree angles.

After being pushed back through the dirt and grasses a few inches, the car and *The Sinful Son* both stopped moving as they both pushed against each other with almost equal force. With powerful footsteps that were like lightning strikes against the land and that broke the ground behind him, along with an exponentially rising power level created by unholy emotions, *The Sinful Son* began to menacingly thud forward unstoppably, slowly pushing the car, which had its gas pedal pressed all the way down.

Realizing that pushing the car all the way to where the four men had been capture would be tiring and practically worthless, Damon switched his grip to the underside of the front of the vehicle while still pushing it back. The agent inside was beginning to panic but feared that abandoning the vehicle would put her in even more danger. As he thudded forward, he began to squat down. Then, with an explosive burst of superhuman strength, *The Sinful Son* flipped the car up, and it stood vertically. Before it could fall back toward him, Damon charged forward and pushed the vehicle so that it landed upside down, the tires spinning chaotically.

"Hmph. So, it would seem that I might have to fight him myself since our agents are capable of handling such a task," the man stated coldly, as if he could kill Damon just by walking toward him. "It's a bother, but it's an easy task that I could accomplish within just a few seconds. I've grown bored of this already, and there's no need for him to continue on. I could send multiple vehicles and agents, but the results will be completely the same. He's unstoppable compared to them. Otherwise, I'd have him crucified right now. I hate getting my own hands dirty, but these agents are pathetic. Even if he got to us, which he will shortly, he could never defeat me or free the others, so his efforts are futile either way." The man took a bold step forward, but he stopped when the woman grabbed his arm.

"As your wife, I would advise against that," the woman stated. "I don't want you hurting any of them, after all, as I do care for them a bit. Besides, there's no need for you to have to do such menial labor when we have an almost endless amount of agents. Sure, he's killed almost a hundred of them, but just a few more feet, and he'll be here. The distance that the agents had to cross to get to him was in his favor, but once he's here, a large number of them could easily overwhelm him."

The Sinful Son ripped off two car doors from the vehicle he had flipped, equipping one to each hand by holding the interior. They served as both defense and offense. He could not hear what the man and woman were quietly talking about, but he knew that he would be running out of time. At a wrathful speed like that of a spreading fire on a windy day during a drought in a forest, *The Sinful Son* rushed forward as a sea of agents charged at him. Using his repurposed car doors to concentrate his raging power to a single point on either arm, *The Sinful Son* smashed, stabbed, back-handed, crushed, chopped in half, smacked away, and killed dozens of agents at a time.

Getting close to the demonic figure was impossible for any regular human, and the agents were just that since their guns were rendered useless against the unstoppable being. Several agents grabbed onto each car door, and their combined strength was enough to rip them away from *The Sinful Son*. Doing so, however, only seemed to make his power drastically increase. His hands now free from holding the car doors, *The Sinful Son* broke bones, choked, threw, ripped, tore, twisted, punched, back-handed, overwhelmed, jabbed, hooked, up-percutted, clapped, smacked, and killed even more agents, on top of kicking, stomping, and crushing.

The number of agents that Damon had defeated in an impossible battle of one man against countless others was uncountable as injured and dead bodies began to litter the ground, but the number of re-inforcements and agents at the disposal of The Organization was far greater than that. Soon, *The Sinful Son* was brought to his knees by an overwhelming number of agents. Together, they managed to tight-ly wrap chains around him that were purposefully designed with his strength and unexpected strength in mind. He was, unfortunately, trapped. Together, the agents carried the tied-up Damon over to the other four scientists, leaning him against the metal ring in between Kronos and Timothy.

The man brushed his deadly hands against one another. "That certainly took quite a while," he commented as he turned and looked at the setting sun, which was halfway beneath the horizon now. "If it gets too dark, this won't be as fun. Of course, being prepared for anything and everything as I always am, I've brought the equipment necessary to create enough light for a whole two acres of land. *The Sinful Son* is more impressive than I thought. If I didn't have a private graveyard for the members of my company, I don't know what I'd do with all of these bodies. A good amount of them will survive, and their injuries will be treated by our medical team, which happens to be the best in the world, but you certainly killed a lot of our agents, Damon. Good for you. Now, I suppose introductions are long overdue by this point."

Timothy, using all of the heroism he had read, watched, listened to, and studied, mustered up the courage to speak. "Right. Who are you, and what do you want from us? How do you know who we are? How did you know that we'd all be here?"

"I figured you'd be the one to ask, young Timothy," the man stated. "After all, John seems to still be in shock, Birch is feeling guilty for his involuntary and unknowing involvement in all of this, Damon is testing to see if he can break those chains and what he'll do when he does, and Kronos, as expected, has a smirk on his face and is most likely plotting something that can almost compete with my lowest level of intelligence. So, the only person left to speak is the failed hero who believes that this is all like some fictional lore he enjoyed as a kid. Now, this here is my wife, whose name has been kept secret from everyone," the man said as he gestured to the woman. "The little girl clinging to my wife's left is my youngest child, Isabel. She's named that because she *is a bell* that will ring in the new ways of the future. Then, there's me, and I shouldn't even waste my breath introducing myself to a bunch of people who will all die shortly, but this is my life's work, and I ought to show y'all the respect you deserve. I'm Ugiene, but I go by Gene, and that's what my wife calls me. Everyone else, however, calls me G.O.D."

"An egotistical bastard like yourself *would* have such a sacrilegious name," Timothy replied. "Who do you think you are, comparing yourself to God, who is the divine creator of the universe?"

"It's not a poke at religion or meant to praise and caress my large ego at all, young Timothy. The pronunciation and spelling are certainly a bit more than coincidental, but I didn't create the title because I believed that I was on the same level as your fictional leader and religious entity. I am the most powerful being to have ever existed, but that doesn't make me as powerful as a fictitious entity that can create and destroy anything. Although I do create life, banish life, bless life, curse life, and take away life. G.O.D. is an acronym standing for Genetics Operation Director. That's what and who I am, as I am the leader of The Genetic Corporation, as well as the father of all five of you men!"

The five men broke out laughing and yelling skeptically at Gene's bold and unbelievable statement.

"Laugh and deny it all you want, but I shall reveal the truth to you here and now. Your entire lives have been lies, and all of you are nothing but disposable researchers for The Genetic Corporation. Just think about how similar all of you are to each other! Don't believe that we've been around that long? Ask John what he knows about us because, like Birch, he's been involved with us. Granted, he didn't know it at the time, but he did exactly what we wanted him to."

His dark eyes almost shadowed over, John looked at Gene with somber realization. "Gene's not lying, guys. A few decades ago, I broke into a building for a company called The Genetic Corporation, and I stole their research on telomeres and telomerase to help me with my efforts to become truly immortal. They've been around for a long time." John clenched his pale hands into fists as he looked at the mask on Gene and the mask on his wife. "In fact, they've been around since World War I and probably earlier than that, because they created the despicable suit and mask that I stole over one century ago. These people are immortal and invulnerable, and their masks seem to work even better than mine, as they look like they're detachable, unlike my permanent one. There's no doubt that they're wearing the suits as well. The only reason Isabel doesn't have one is that they're waiting for her to stop growing."

Gene clapped slowly and condescendingly as he nodded his head with a bit of pride. "Well, aren't you brighter than everyone thinks. I know you five men don't believe a word I've said yet, but you'll find that I am the only person alive who knows every truth of this world. My journey started back in America during the late mid-1800s when I was born as a superhumanly smart human being. My intelligence greatly impressed people. The priest believed that I was a prophet. I continued to grow smarter with each day that passed, discovering new things, and helping out the local towns. I'm just glad they didn't hang me on account of believing I was a witch or something supernatural.

After meeting my wife, the two of us moved out to the western part of America to work on advancing science faster than anyone else. She, like myself, was highly intelligent, and I knew she was more than just a pretty woman the moment I first saw her."

"We fell in love because we knew that no one would be able to stop us when we put our two minds together," the woman stated. "The seclusiveness of our new home was quite helpful, and we quickly began to advance in ways that you would all find unbelievable. Then, when the war happened, that really distracted everyone from what we were doing. None of the technology, inventions, or scientific breakthroughs were impressive to us until we discovered D.N.A. It sounds unbelievable, but we discovered it before anyone else and kept it a secret. That was what changed everything for us. We didn't care about technology or inventions, because those only helped humans with their lives and to cope with their weaknesses. Instead, we decided and realized that we wanted to improve humans biologically. That would be far more efficient than just improving current technology and inventions, as well as better than creating new stuff for society."

Gene nodded his head. "For the next few decades, we would laugh at the scientists who raced and fought to model the shape of D.N.A. They were nothing compared to us, and they never would be anything but the public's declaration of a truth that we had discovered and kept hidden decades ago. In fact, they were ages behind our advancements, and we had been studying D.N.A. around-the-clock in order to improve humans on a biological level, and one day, on a genetic level that could easily be manipulated."

"However, there's more to the story than just that," the woman pointed out. "Through our rigorous researching and constant devotion to our unbelievable work in the shadows of society, we learned about and discovered molecules and atoms. After studying the behavior and properties of those particles, we realized the danger that might occur if other great minds learned what we knew, and what people might try to do with that knowledge. Nuclear weapons, for example. So, we kept the new discoveries to ourselves. Unfortunately, however, time was running out for both of us. We were aging, as all humans naturally do."

"Appalled by that fact, you decided to see if you could use atoms as a way to protect people from external factors that accelerate and affect aging," John stated gravely. "Isn't that right? You created the suit and mask as a way to slow down aging. While it wasn't perfect immortality, it was a start that would provide you with enough time to figure out how to fix your aging problem permanently."

Gene applauded proudly. "That's right, Johnny-boy. Before any of that, however, my wife and I had sex and gave birth to our first son, which is you. We then sent you away. After that, we created prototypes and used them on others, and it took quite a while until we had a product that was worthy. See, the suits and masks were permanent, as that was the best we could do during that time. We understood that would mean no more children, so we continued studying genetics and reproduction. After seeing John's progress with the suit and mask, and having collected and safely stored almost endless samples of our sperm and egg, we put on the suits. We left the masks off until we could make a kind that was detachable, allowing us to function like regular people for the most part, while also allowing us to breathe the air of this world a few times a year to help our immune system catalog the new diseases of this planet."

"You're getting ahead of yourself, Gene," the woman said to Gene before turning to the five capture men. "See, his intelligence is unrivaled, and it always has been. That led him to boredom, and he lost his passion for learning and creating. Until, he came up with an idea and a project that was bigger than anything we had ever done or even thought of, and the blazing fire of his passion was reignited."

Gene took a step toward the men. "This shall be the revelation that clarifies everything. Starting with John, I began my biggest project: a game to see how intelligent I was while also providing me with benefits. Nothing was beyond my comprehension. I accounted for every variable, could predict any outcome, and I knew everything. People, however, can be the most unpredictable. Not common folk, as I knew every societal trend and pattern in human behavior, but advanced individuals that were new to society… well, they would be far more difficult to understand, manipulate, and predict. One individual like that would have multiple unknown variables and unpredictable behavior, but I wanted more than that. The bigger the scale, the more difficult it would be, and, in turn, the more interesting and fun it would be. So, using our knowledge of D.N.A., sperm, eggs, genetics, and reproduction, we figured out that we could predetermine and choose how our children would be from now on. It was the earliest form of genetic editing. Using that, I would create unique individuals and then send them out into the world, placing them into the families, areas, and situations that would push them to be their strongest and smartest. Manipulating so many lives on such a large scale was the exciting part of the game, but the best part was that you would all make extraordinary breakthroughs that I could then steal for myself. Not only that, but individuals with *my* genes would be the *best* challenge."

Timothy, shocked and disgusted by what he had heard, quickly shook and struggled to escape the metal ring. "You're telling me that you created us just to see if you could predict our futures based on our genetics and personality when placed into a predetermined family and situation? That's despicable and sickening! That's completely inhumane and immoral. That's abuse of science and the creation of life. I don't believe a word you say, to be honest. Even if it's true, why end the game now?"

"Well, that's because I'm no longer the only player. I would have continued this game forever, but it grew larger than I thought. Unique individuals other than you five have been popping up from thin air, and they've interfered with your lives. Controlling so many people, situations, and variables on such a large scale has almost entirely drained the resources of The Genetic Corporation, as well as become almost impossible. Then, as I said, I'm not the only player anymore. I have my rival, which is Kronos, as he was suspicious of me and was beginning to change everything. He began to connect all of you together, and that ruined the game. Until I used him to end the game. His intelligence is worthy of my respect and honor."

"I appreciate the praise since *I'm* the most intelligent person to have ever existed, but I'm a bit skeptical myself," Kronos said. "If what you say is true, how did you know that we would become scientists and make these breakthroughs? No one can determine a future like that just based on genetics, let alone for five people. That's not even accounting for personalities, which are slightly predictable but not entirely. Plus, there are unpredictable natural incidents and the introduction of other people into our lives, just to name a few uncontrollable variables. Just for one person, accounting, analyzing, and predicting so many variables would be almost impossible."

"That's true, Kronos, but difficult and impossible are not the same, especially when you have as many resources as I do. Don't forget that I've been around for almost two centuries. I knew everything about you, so that made it a lot easier. I genetically created you using my sperm and my wife's eggs. Your heights are all what I chose. Your eyes are all what I chose. Your hair, skin, penis size, weight, lung capacity, bone density, and everything about you were all *created* and monitored by *me*! *I* gave you the genetic mutation to have denser bones, Kronos. *I* designed Timothy to have the exactly perfect build for running. *I* increased the amount of growth hormones Birch would have, and *I* gave him his myostatin-related muscular hypertrophy. Do you understand that *I'm* in control?"

"I understand that you like to hear yourself talk and that you also like to praise yourself," Kronos replied. "Perhaps that's where I get it from. It's true that you've created us genetically and knew our bodies better than we did, but that still doesn't explain our personalities. Some studies suggest that personality can partially be the result of genetics, but personalities are also influenced and changed by our experiences and the people in our lives."

"*Both* of which *I* controlled. We've been tracking all five of you since day one of your creations, eavesdropping with listening-devices and spying with surveillance equipment. We've heard and seen almost everything. In fact, we've even used live people to spy on all of you. Our agents are *everywhere*, including some of your neighbors, but it's not just common folk either. Dr. Finch is one of the top members of our company, and y'all went and ate one of his buildings. Both of your servants are spies, Kronos. Laura Godwin's best friend is an agent, Hanna who volunteers at the gym is an agent, Morgan from our military base is an agent, and the list goes on for quite a while. I've been planning everything out for decades, manipulating everything that affected your lives to create the strongest version of you possible. We control more external factors than you think, and while we don't control everything, we have been a part of the most major parts of your life."

"Listen, all of you just need to be patient. Our story is a long one, but now, I'll go one by one and explain," the woman said as she walked toward them. "We'll be here forever if I tried to name every variable in your life that we controlled or manipulated, but I'll name enough so that you understand that we're telling the truth. I *am* your mother, and Gene is the ultimate lifeform and your father."

The five men were enraged, sorrowful, doubtful, curious, and they had no choice, trapped as they were, but to listen to the man and woman who claimed to be their creators.

The woman walked over to John first, who seemed to be just an empty carcass behind the suit and mask. His dark eyes were hollow shadows, and his silent breath seemed to be the air of a stagnant day as he stared forward into the past. "Don't look so down, John. You're the only child of mine to have actually been created inside of my body, and so my connection with you is far stronger than these other people. You might think I'm lying, but I hated seeing you suffer for all of your life, and I wanted to be there for you when you were suffering from depression, but my calling to G.O.D., my husband, is far greater than that. It's nothing personal, and you should be proud to know that you're Mommy's favorite."

Slowly raising his head like a paralyzed man on his deathbed, John looked up at the woman, not recognizing anything about her. He did not remember her or Gene. All he knew and all he had ever known were his alcoholic father and his cold mother in Cape Cod. "Please… I need to know something. It's important to me because I realize now that I should have listened to her. Ava… is she an agent for your vile company?"

"Rest easy, John. She is just a girl who happened to wander into your life. Well, we knew you would meet her. We also knew that despite your depression and suicidal thoughts, you would want to achieve full immortality after stealing the suit and mask, which were practically given to you by our agents during the war. We knew you would become, as Kronos has nicknamed you, The Immortalizer. A powerful name, but even more so is the name we gave you. I thought of this one, as you're my favorite. I decided to name you John Leach since you leech off of life and cheat death. Well, you leech off of the technology that others created, and you were going to do that today as well." The hollow shadows that were John's eyes emptied out a few tears. "So, we gave you an alcoholic father and a wrathful mother who was sick, as Gene knew those were best for what he wanted to do."

"Damn it! So, you're the creators of the suit and mask?" John asked bitterly through clenched teeth behind the darkness of his mask. "I've spent my whole life wondering who you were and whether or not you still existed. I could never imagine what they would be like, and you're not at all what I would have ever expected."

"I know, sweetie, and I'm sorry that you're disappointed. It doesn't end there, though. We let you steal our research on telomeres and telomerase, which we had been making excellent progress on. Letting you be the test subject for immortality was the wisest decision. Brace yourself now because it gets worst. We killed Kyle! He was a nice enough man and a brilliant doctor, but he had to die. We recently updated the maps online to allow you to make some connections, and then Morgan led you to the base, and you were allowed to get on that jet to get here. The worst part, however, was when we had to kill Carly Rossi. It broke my heart that we had to kill my firstborn son's first love, but it was a crucial step in creating your personality and setting up your goals."

Unable to stay strong or lifeless, John cried as a waterfall burst forward from each of his dark eyes. He clenched his teeth and his fists as he struggled against the metal ring with sorrowful rage. "*No!* How could someone be so *cruel?* How could you kill her? You murdered her! She was innocent and perfect, and you murdered her for your stupid game because you're selfish! You murdered Kyle!" He screamed out in rage and agony, but it was useless. "How can you be so heartless and inhuman? How could you involve innocent people in your *despicable* experiment?"

"Well, there's a simple answer for that, and it's the fact that the future our goals shall create greatly outweighs the cost of a few lives. My husband and I have big plans for the world."

"You make me *sick*," John spat out. He shook with bitterness. "No matter what happens here today, I'll *kill both* of you. My depression and suicidal thoughts were the result of the life you made me endure, but now that I've met you, I'm a changed man. All I have left is bitterness and a burning desire for revenge. You killed me emotionally, and you murdered the only people in my life that I ever cared about. It's unforgivable! I'll continue to live, and I'll hunt you down across the *entire* world. I'll chase you from state to state, from country to country, and from continent to continent. Equipped with invulnerability and immortality, nothing will stop me from hunting you down, and then, I shall kill you."

"You're pathetic, John, and I take back what I said about you being my favorite," the woman said coldly as she walked over to where Gene was standing, a stern and unreadable expression on his face. "Your threat has hurt my feelings. However, I shall disregard what you said and continue on with my story of truths as quickly as I can. I've waited decades for this moment, but I want to get home before it gets dark, and the sun is almost gone. See, you weren't just my favorite, John, and your D.N.A. led to some troubles amongst The Genetic Corporation."

"*Good*," John retorted. "I'm glad it caused you trouble, because that's what you people deserve, and that's being fully merciful. What does my D.N.A. have to do with it, though?"

"Hmph," Gene sounded in wrathful disappointment. "We had a rogue agent. It's only happened once, and we took care of the situation, but he caused quite a lot of trouble. Every agent is now loyal to me, and they always will be, but even money and fear did not stop him. A man was obsessed with you for reasons that we still don't know or understand, but he let it consume him. Whether it was your genes, appearance, personality, lifestyle, or whatever it was that captivated him, he loved you. However, he hated homosexuals, so he devised a plan to make you his without breaking his morals. We have countless samples of D.N.A. stored from each of you five. Aware of that, the man stole some of yours and tried to make a clone of you. During the cloning process, he attempted to switch out pieces of the genetic code to change your gender, but it resulted in horrible results. He wasn't smart enough to do it properly, and he accidentally allowed other genes to mix in."

The woman shook her head in disappointment. "The result was a female human that you all know as Francesca Leach. She was mentally unstable and an unwanted side effect of our failure to stop the rogue agent. So, I named her Mallory, which is based in French roots and essentially means unfortunate one, which is the perfect way to describe that witch. She was the first girl we made, but I don't consider that freak my daughter. Isabel is my one and only daughter." She wrapped her left arm around Isabel, who clung to her mother's left leg. "Mallory Leach has the same last name as you because she is, in a way, your direct sister, John. She leeches off of others and their pain."

"*You foul and most impure creature!*" Damon bellowed, a few agents flinching and backing away. "*Why not prevent her from enduring the endless suffering that she would live through by ending her life as soon as it began? How could you allow her to live, knowing that she would be a menace to society who, like a parasite, leeched off of innocent people, breaking others and tearing apart their families?*" Calling upon the unholy power of T*he Sinful Son*, which was growing with his disbelief and rage, Damon flexed and pressed against the chains that bound him, but they had been specifically designed to keep him trapped.

The woman cackled. "Struggle and yell like a barbarian all you want, but you won't be able to break those, Damon," the woman stated half-faithfully as the metal chains creaked and a few even cracked.

"We kept her, Damon, because I had already planned ahead, and I knew that we needed her for you. She needed someone to help her, and you needed a woman. A good woman would have kept you Damon, but Mallory helped unleash **The Sinful Son**. It was actually more interesting to keep her alive. It was like I had been thrown a curveball by that rogue agent. It's like I was playing chess, but he pulled out a special piece that only he had. After defeating him, I obtained that piece, but it didn't match my set, and it was difficult to use. That made my game all the more interesting. The year she was made was also a time of recovery and growth for us, because I realized that I still wasn't being challenged enough. John lived such a predictable and monotonous life that manipulating him was too easy. Not to mention, his isolation and lack of leaving his home made it even easier. I was growing bored, and I need someone more unpredictable and unique."

"Based on your description and my guess of how old Mallory was, I assume you're talking about me," Kronos stated. "After all, I am the most unique person to have ever existed, so there's no doubt that you're referring to me."

Gene's stern face lit up with ill and selfish satisfaction and pride as he took a step toward Kronos. "That's right, my boy. In fact, you're my favorite creation ever, and I mean out of *everything*. Kids are usually about half of each of their parents, although physical appearance or personality tends to lean one way or the other. You, however, were created to be as similar to me as possible. You're not charming or handsome like I am, but your massive intelligence is just like mine. Not only that, but you're a man of many secrets and plans, just as I am."

"It makes me happy to see daddy so happy and proud," Isabel told her mother.

"Me too, sweetie," the woman replied to Isabel. A bit of envy in her gaze, along with some maternal love, she turned toward Kronos. "We actually raised you for a few years in Greece before we sent you off. That photo you have is fake, of course. Sir Thomas, although not an agent of our company, worked for us quite favorably. His personality was the perfect balance for yours, at least in the way we needed it to be."

"That's right," Gene said. "After all, you are our star pupil. I made you with the intention of possibly fearing you one day. Instead of playing this game by myself, I made you as a rival for me to compete against. If you managed to learn of us or suspect us enough, well, that would've been *really* interesting. Granted, you've all made scientific breakthroughs that are remarkable, but Kronos has done better than all of you other individuals put together. *Better*, but not the best. Whether purposeful or accidental, he got sick from self-experimentation, and that devalues him a bit. Then again, so did you, Birch and Timothy. In a way, John has been suffering from the suit and mask experiment his entire life. Mallory's failure to fix herself and the use of her knowledge to fuel her addiction led to her downfall. Then, there's Damon, who will die internally from his own source of power.

"As always, my husband's observation is correct," the woman stated as she shook her head, ashamed and disappointed. "You've all brought about your own doom, and that's just the general statement. It's quite a shame actually, to know that all scientists die sick in the story we created as a book for Gene to read and manipulate. I mean, we knew that you would all end up sick, but it still breaks my heart to know that *I*, your own loving mother, did this to all of you."

Gene nodded his head. "Your inevitable sickness is actually why I named you Kronos Nephus, son," Gene stated proudly. "Your body is consuming its own brain cells just as the titan Kronos consumed his own children in Greek Mythology. People argue over the spelling, but a creator as powerful as myself can't worry about such a tedious thing. Your last name, Nephus, is a term meaning you are a god's son and destined to be a god yourself. How about that?" Gene chuckled earnestly.

"I can't help but feel satisfied by all of the compliments you two have given me," Kronos stated as he looked at Gene, trying to understand his true father. "However, as a man of logic, reason, and evidence-based facts, I'm afraid I still don't believe you entirely. I understand that the money, castle, and Sir Thomas all provided me with certain opportunities, but you still can't predict and make emotions or a person's personality, even with your resources."

"That's where you're wrong, Kronos. We *can* determine human emotion for the most part, and we do know how it will affect people. Even an individual as unique as yourself shares some common behavioral patterns with regular humans." Gene looked past Kronos at an agent and summoned him forward. "Isn't that right, Mark?"

From the crowd of agents stepped forward a man who walked over to Kronos, a smug expression on his face. It was Mark, the juvenile punk who had stolen Annabelle from Kronos decades ago. "Well, well, well," he said mockingly. "If it isn't little Kronos Nephus, the scientist. It looks like I won in the end! I never even cared about that dumb bitch. I just had to steal her from you and then fight you during that stupid hurricane. Unfortunately, G.O.D. can't predict where fucking lightning is going to strike," Mark snarled as he removed his sunglasses, showing more of his lightning-scarred face. "So, to make you suffer and pay for what happened to me, I'm going to be the one who kills you tonight. Not only that, but I think I'll take these as well," Mark said smugly as he pulled the high-tech sunglasses off of Kronos' face and put them on. "Free technology like this is priceless, and I can't wait to kill you while wearing these, because irony like that makes revenge even more enjoyable," Mark hissed as he taunted Kronos.

Kronos, however, smirked. "Hmm. That last thing you just said is technically an opinion. Therefore, I cannot say that it is either correct or incorrect, but your statement claiming that you won in the end is actually a fact that can be debated. As the smartest person here, I'll inform you that it is *incorrect*! *I*, **King Kronos**, shall be the one to win in the end, because I always do. Venomous-Injection-Code," Kronos commanded the high-tech sunglasses.

Responding to the command, the high-tech sunglasses injected lethal venom into Mark. He looked into Kronos' amber-yellow eyes in shock before collapsing to the ground. Using the last of his strength, Mark pulled out his cellphone and whispered something into it before dying almost instantly.

After gesturing to a few agents to move Mark's body, Gene slowly shook his head, disappointed in Mark and proud of Kronos. "Accounting for variables, theorizing, and predicting are all major factors that separate the smart from the stupid," Gene preached to all of the agents that were within the range of his powerful voice. "An intelligent person would not equip the gear of an enemy on them, and that is especially the case when your enemy is the second most intelligent human to have ever existed. That injection of venom killed Mark almost instantly. He did not experience pain, meaning that the injection was not a defense against intruders, but rather, it was a suicidal function Kronos made in case he was captured or in a truly desperate situation. Mark got what he deserved. Let this be a lesson to you all."

A majority of the agents, however, were not listening. They were shocked by what had just happened. Mark's death, combined with all of the corpses **The Sinful Son** had left behind before he was captured, struck fear into the hearts of the regular people. Their faith in G.O.D. was the only thing keeping them from running away, and so was their fear of him and his endless intelligence that had been growing for almost two centuries. They knew that death was the preferable option, for there was no escaping The Genetic Corporation.

Isabel was the only one to shed tears over Mark's death, and she buried her face into her mother's leg.

"Even knowing that was coming, I was shocked by it. I had hoped he would be smarter than that. Anyhow, allow me to finish explaining everything before anything else dramatic happens. I know a man such as yourself needs more evidence, Kronos, and I'm sure your remaining brothers are interested in knowing how I manipulated their lives as well. John is more lifeless than ever, and you seem to be taking all of these revelations as if you already knew all of them, which is impossible." Gene chuckled. "Quite honestly, you didn't even seem that surprised when you found out that Mark was working for us, but I guess you're just happy to have beat him in the end. It's a shame that you never ended up with Annabelle. I would've been happy for you two."

"A lie, but I'll treat it as a sentimental remark," Kronos said. "I'm rather curious about how else you manipulated my life to try and improve my perfect self. Is Robert an agent of your company?"

"Not at all, but his son will be very useful if we experience problems in the future. Chief Whallington is a good man and a good cop, but he is of no value to us. We did help him pull strings to get those prisoners you needed for the test subjects, and the other people you experimented on were agents of our company who were willing to sacrifice their health for the greater good. We also framed Jack, but that's not entirely important. Honestly, in comparison to the others, you've been influenced and manipulated by us the least. Except for Mark and what happened with Annabelle, there wasn't a need for us to interfere. You were already the man we needed you to be, and given your isolation and personality, changing you wouldn't have been hard."

"Interesting," Kronos stated. That was all he had to say on the matter, as he was preoccupied with his own thoughts.

"Fast forward five years from your birth, Kronos, and we create twins," Gene stated proudly. "Damon Willow and Birch Willow. Two giants, but one is far more superior in physical size. You know, I was going to give the bone mutation to Birch instead of you, Kronos. That would have made him unstoppable and a real-life superhuman, capable of withstanding almost any physical attack. However, I decided to give it to you. That said, Birch was made to be a superhuman. A man who would grow fond of nature, I named him after two types of trees. That's all there is to his name, as I realized that names are just names at the end of the day. The only thing else that can be said is that willow trees just go with the flow and are peaceful. The name Damon is close sounding to demon, and so that was the reasoning behind his name."

The woman walked over to Birch, who just seemed depressed by all that had been revealed. "Don't look so down, Birch. I hate seeing you sad," the woman said earnestly. "I've always really admired your heart and spirit, because you are *so* strong emotionally. Actually, I always donated at your charity events, because it was the only way I could help you out. I know that you were created for Gene to be challenged and so that we could reap the benefits of your research and experiments, but I'm really impressed by all that you did while you were alive. You touched the lives of so many people. Oh, and when Rose died," the woman's voice was truly sympathetic and hurt, "my heart broke with yours."

"That's enough," Gene stated coldly. "I was going to leave you out of this operation, but you promised me you could handle this. You wanted to just steal their research and let them live the rest of their lives. Perhaps, it's because you're their mother and have a love for them that I don't, but we cannot forget why we are doing this, as well as the future that will be created following the events of today. Stop being so caring. Is that understood?"

"Of course, Gene," the woman replied bitterly. "Anyway, Birch, we manipulated your life a bit too. It was our agents who ran the orphanage you were at and allowed you to escape. We even sent Abraham to work with you, because he really admired you and was wowed by everything you did. Through him, we helped you create your gym. We let those bears loose at that town picnic. We sent an agent posing as a rude truck driver your way. We knocked all of these trees down and had an agent pose as a cop to shut the road down. All of the farmers who rent out your land are agents. That woman you helped wasn't an agent, but one was with her. Sorry about your friend Michael, but we need him for our own purposes. Oh, and I'm really sorry about what we did to that cow of yours. I know how much you loved him."

Birch was crying, and he sobbed softly. His heart was truly broken. When he spoke, it was a gruff whisper as he stared at the dirt and grasses in front of him, his head hung low. "Earlier, John said that y'all make him *sick*. That's exactly how I feel. Your selfishness is sickening. Tuh think that you would endanger the lives o' innocent people and make us suffer for ya own gain is sickening, because I try not tuh believe that such evilness exists in the world, let alone in the hearts of humans. You hurt animals. You hurt others. You hurt me. You hurt muh families. Still, I'll be comforted if you answer this one question."

"Of course, sweetie," the woman said empathetically as she walked over to Birch. "I'm sorry that all of this has to happen to you. You're a kind person who would never want to hurt others like this. So, if I can comfort you, as unbelievable as it seems, that would make me feel better."

Sniffling his nose strongly, Birch tilted his head up to look at the woman through his helmet. "Rose wasn't an agent, was she? You didn't kill her, did you?"

"No," the woman replied somberly as she slowly shook her head. "She wasn't an agent. Her disease was the result of a genetic mutation, but it had nothing to do with us. She was a good girl, and I'm sorry that you had to see her die so young."

"You have my wife's condolences, Birch. I couldn't care less about what happened in your life, as I'm just concerned with who you are now. Your physical strength impresses me, and setting everything up so you and Michael would meet was perfectly planned, as your body combines well with the power of cellulose digestion. Then, there's your twin brother, who is a biological weapon that the world has never seen the likes of before." Gene stepped closer to Damon and then stopped, staying a few feet away from him.

"It would appear that even you are not brave, for it is obvious to us all that you are afraid," Damon stated aggressively.

All of the agents gasped.

Gene had a smug smirk on his face, hidden behind his mask. "Is that what you truly think? It's not that at all. I'm being smart. I know for a fact that the agents of my company are some of the brightest in the world, but they've underestimated all of you. That's why Mark is dead, along with all of the people you killed. They made those chains specifically with your strength in mind, but *The Sinful Son* is more powerful than they know. If I get any closer, you'll create a storm of black smoke and chemicals before busting out of those chains. As soon as you're free, you'll either attack me, kill Isabel, or run away and save yourself. No matter what you would choose to do, I can't allow any of those to happen."

The Sinful Son chuckled maniacally. "*Exactly so, for these chains are not of hindrance. Either way, the distance between us makes no difference. A man of truths, you have not lied, but I assure you that Isabel shall die. Not by my own hand, for I fear she is innocent in all of this, but she shall be crushed by giant fists. Smart? There is no doubt that your intelligence is unrivaled, but there is so much more to survival. My strength does far exceed the expectation of these weaklings, and with the unholy truths you've revealed, my powers are peaking. I can break these chains as you have observed while I rhyme, but I am merely waiting for the proper time. Damon was forced into submission by The Sinful Son during an unholy vision, all due to a family of monsters that lacked morals, and now I know that I shall see tomorrow. As the family of wickedness that I was forced to suffer through was all because of you,*" Damon stated as his artificial red eyes seemed to blaze more powerfully than before at Gene.

Isabel ran over and hugged Gene's leg, gripping it tightly as she held on for dear life. "Daddy!" Isabel said through tears. "What is that monster talking about? Am I going to die? What do you have to do with this? Is he going to hurt you?"

"Are you questioning my power?" Gene asked coldly, reinforcing into his daughter's mind the idea that he was the ultimate lifeform and unbeatable. "Go stay with your mother. She'll protect you while I deal with your brothers for their misbehavior. He's not going to try hurting me, and he wouldn't be able to, okay? Now go!"

"***Now that she has returned to that woman who follows you blindly and without question, I suppose it's time to talk about my fake family of oppression that gave me a raging depression and taught me many a lesson. Cruel father of mine, more human than the fake monster who raised me, answer my questions right away, and perhaps I'll allow you to die in a painless way***," Damon stated severely, revenge encompassing him like an aura of fire. "***What did you do to manipulate my life? Did you have society stab me in the back with a knife? That day I died and was devoured by the darkness of death, were you the one to restore my breath? Was Francesca truly what was needed for The Sinful Son to break out and run?***"

Gene nodded his head. "She was the ultimate piece of the puzzle that formed the menacing picture of ***The Sinful Son***. We did save your life that day you killed yourself, but we already had matching blood ready for you, as well as the best medical professionals and supplies around. No one else would have allowed Francesca, some random woman, to be a part of the medical team helping save your life. You cut yourself twice on each wrist, diagonally away from your thumbs. I remember that, as it was rather intriguing, and I'm sure you still have the scars. See, I, G.O.D., personally resurrected ***The Sinless Son*** to ensure that you would become ***The Sinful Son***. Besides that, we ensure you grew up miserably, and we set everything up so you would eventually help save the broken. There are more specific examples from your life, but," Gene looked behind him, "the sun's about to be completely gone."

"So, it's my turn then, right?" Timothy's voice was different. It had matured, and it was filled with defiance and determination, as well as backed by justice and righteousness.

Gene, smirking to himself, walked over to Timothy. "Well, if it isn't young Timothy. Known as Timothy Edward Godwin, your name spells 'Time God' when you take certain letters away and squish the remaining ones together. We're just going to skip over Damon? How rude. You sound awfully determined to prove us all wrong, and I admire that. I'm disappointed, though. I failed this game in one part, as I had predicted that you would remain pure-hearted and that Birch would be corrupted by his emotions. Yet, here we are, and it's the exact opposite of what I had predicted. That's not how the story was supposed to go, but sometimes, characters just write themselves, and that was the interesting part about this game. However, your life has been an intriguing one for me, as I was around *long* before comic books and heroes were a thing. I've never really been into them. You, on the other hand, are obsessed with that crap. In fact, you'll try and be a hero to the very end. I can hear it in your voice."

"I *am* a hero, and your defeat is inevitable. Not only that, but I'm not your son. None of us are your kids, and I can prove it!" The other four men turned toward Timothy as best as they could, shocked at his bold statement. "I'll save all of us with solid evidence that proves you're lying, and that you're just trying to manipulate us."

"Is that so?" Gene, his face stern again, was not at all shocked or intimidated by the statement. "Then go ahead and tell me what that might be."

"I, Timothy Edward Godwin, am a hero, and I took a D.N.A. test a few years ago that proves you wrong. My hatred for my mother made me hope that perhaps she was not my mother after all, and so I took a genetic test to see if she was actually related to me. The results came back with a family tree that had both my father and mother on it, and it even showed how much we were related and what we had genetically in common. So, through the power of science, I have proven you wrong."

"That is correct, but *I'm* the one who made that family tree. How truthful do you honestly believe those genetic tests to be? At the end of the day, it's just some company telling you who you're related to, and, because they say they tested and matched your genes, you believe them. The person in charge could tell five random people, who are somewhat similar, that they are all related if they all took a genetic test at that company, and those five people would all believe it because they have no way of proving that the company is right or wrong. They choose to believe that companies are moral and ethical and that their scientific reports are true and not lies all strung together. The Genetic Corporation created your family tree, Timothy, as well as you and your life. We had a false family tree and genetic test ready for all five of you. I am G.O.D. No one can stop me. So just give it a rest with your heroic talk. At the end of the day, you aren't helping anyone."

"The Genetic Corporation, huh? That's what your company is called after two centuries of planning?" Timothy spat at the ground. "Well, that's a bland name if you ask me. It's completely cliche and tacky. You guys suck."

"Bash and criticize our company name all you want before you die sick, but it, like everything in my life, was done for a specific reason beyond the comprehension of most. Our name is generic so that we don't stick out. We're going to take over this land, and all other countries slowly, from the inside out. We don't want to be some big-name company just yet. It draws too much attention. Once we have taken over, which we have already begun to do so in America, it will be delightful."

"Wrong! It won't be delightful, because your company is built on the suffering of others as well as blood," Timothy yelled. "I'll admit that I'm a failed hero, but you are a truly despicable villain."

"Is that what you think, Timothy? Is that what *all five* of you are thinking right now? It's incorrect! You all think that you're the hero and main character of this story? That I'm the villain who suddenly showed up at the end like a plot twist and ruined your lives? Well, you're wrong, and believing that you're the main character and hero of your own life is a tragic sin, because it's self-centered, narcissistic, unheroic, and nothing but negative traits. A hero like you should have known that, Timothy. I don't expect you or any of your idiot brothers to understand, though, because you're all the bad guys. You're all the villains, and you were always meant to just disappear without helping the world."

"You're wrong," Timothy cried out desperately, refusing and not wanting to believe what Gene was saying.

"I'm not wrong, Timothy. The Genetic Corporation has been researching and discovering cures for diseases and even some cancers for decades. We've anonymously made medical breakthroughs that changed the world. Our latest research and inventions will, after the events here today, help more people than R.O.M.A.B.A. Industries has. We've improved the health of more people than Birch's gym ever would have. All of our technology is clean renewable energy. It's not just how good we are but also how terrible you all are. Kronos is an egomaniac who has no regard for civilians, society, property damage, public peace, or even the people close to him, and he's a liar and manipulator. Timothy is a vigilante who hospitalized a firefighter and negatively affects people's bodies to create his illusions, and then there's his whole Florida incident. Not to mention, he hit his own mother. John has killed a lot of people just because they were in his way, he broke Ava's heart, and he tried to kill himself and wasted the decades granted to him by the research that he stole. Damon fights for the broken but considers everyone else horrible and is a killer who exists in a constant state of utter rage. Francesca tortured people and did horrible things, as well as treated the only man who cared for her like he was worthless. And for such a nice guy, Birch stole from his partner behind his back and self-experimented. Besides that, he made a deal with shady people to create his gym when he knew that it was wrong. My wife said that all scientists die sick in this story that I've created, and that's the ending of the game, unfortunately, but it's not just physically. You're all sick socially, mentally, and emotionally."

The five men all wanted to deny those facts and shout that Gene was wrong and that he was truly the villain, but they all lowered their heads in shame instead. Unfortunately, in their hearts, they knew that everything he had stated was undeniable.

Gene laughed contemptuously. He narrowed his eyes as his face hardened with intimidating disapproval. "That's what I thought. Your silence proves me correct because only fools would verbally persist against the undeniable truth. Were you all trying to help and do the right thing? I believe that in a way, you were trying to be good, but your intentions were all self-ish ones: attention, power, speed, strength, fame, entertainment, money, fear, pleasure, egotism, and a whole plethora of negative reasons. It's why you'll all die sick and corrupted by your own personalities."

"The personalities *you* created," Timothy pointed out, unwilling to submit to Gene, his intelligence, and his truths.

"Well, you got me there," Gene said with a laugh as shrugged off the verbal jab. "Your persistence is a bit admirable, but enough of this blame-game, however. I won't stand here all day discussing such trivial philosophies with you. There's much for me to do after I kill all five of you and steal everything you've ever researched, worked on, and created. Thank you for your decades of service to our company. I just wanted you all to know that The Genetic Corporation is on Earth's side and that we shall save humanity and improve everyone's lives, creating a society where a majority of the people are truly happy and at peace. They will praise us as heroes."

"You're wrong, Gene," Timothy replied. "Maybe you're right, and everything will work out for the better, but you won't win in the end. Even if everything you say is true, I know, or rather I believe, that the heinous deeds you have committed will one day come back and tear down the empire you are creating. Someday... somehow... the truth about you and your company will be discovered or exposed, destroying it all. Eventually, your immortality will fade to nothing, and no one will remember you or anything good that you did."

Empowered by Timothy's sense of justice, Birch came back to his senses, and he looked toward Gene. "As horrible as all of this is, I agree with muh younger brother, and I have hope. Whether it's through God, the universe, fate, or humans themselves, the evil here tuhday will eventually be exposed and destroyed. I believe that, and I'll try muh best tuh make sure it happens."

Kronos nodded his head and smirked. "Correct."

"And I already told you that I'll use my immortality to hunt you down to the final days of this grim planet," John stated coldly.

"Then, it would seem that all five us agree that the collapse and destruction of your empire burns within all of our hearts like a raging fire. The good of this world, the morals, and justice shall uphold, and one day, the unholy truths of your company shall be exposed, and all will know that your company must go. It is written. It is so. To ensure that such a fate happens regardless of my unfortunate demise," Damon broke the chains around him in an explosive display of strength as he jumped up, *"I shall free my captured brothers with hope shining within their eyes."*

"How are you going to do that? We're unbeatable with G.O.D. at our side," the woman stated as she glared at Damon, holding Isabel close to her leg. Her expression, however, turned to utter terror as she saw a figure appear on the roof of the R.O.M.A.B.A. Industries building. The silhouette walked forward ominously, a black robotic shadow. "All agents, aim your weapons at that figure," the woman commanded with a point toward the roof. "Hold your fire until I say so."

"Why so pale and afraid of that figure, if you were so sure that you would be the winner? I thought you accounted for every variable, including the unknown, but that's not what your expression has shown. I am The Sinful Son, and only I am the one to declare and guarantee when I shall cease to exist, and now prepare for a barrage of fists," Damon exclaimed with a maniacal laugh of unstoppable power and intimidation. The agents nearby cowered, shifting their aim between him and the figure on the roof. He glared at his mother, his red eyes ablaze with revenge and rage, along with a bloodlust that had not been there before.

"Shit! Everyone, fire away," the woman ordered with another point at the figure on the roof.

It was too late.

The ominous figure on the building lifted their cylindrical arms up and then thrust them forward. Following this pattern, the giant metal ring was raised up and then thrown into a group of agents. About twenty of them were knocked down, half of them crushed by the hunk of metal. Birch's helmet and Damon's body followed this pattern, floating up and then soaring a few feet through the air away from the building. The bullets that had been fired at the figure were sent back toward their shooters, killing several agents. The silhouette disappeared from the fight and never came back, feeling that tonight's battle was not their fight. They had done what a paranoid Damon had requested them to do just before his departure to England.

Instantly, chaos broke loose as it became an all-out battle for freedom as the five men now fought against the seemingly endless hordes of agents.

The woman quickly called for backup, calling for every agent and member of The Genetic Corporation to come and fight. She called several over to her and Isabel for protection.

Timothy quickly helped Kronos onto his feet. "Well, talk about a plot twist... we're brothers, I guess." Kronos half-smiled at the remark, quickly shooting past Timothy. The D.O.O.M. Shooter beam went clear through an agent, leaving a gaping hole in the middle of his torso. Then moving the beam left to right, avoiding his other brothers, Kronos cut down several agents at a time. "This is some crazy shit going on," Timothy commented as he took down a few agents with his Whip-Watch. "So, based on what I know, we all have similar genes. While we all have different mutations and certain genes that not all of us have, we're all siblings, and our parents are those bastards over there."

"I understand all of that, so there's no need for you to explain it to me. What's your point, Timothy?" Kronos asked as he choked a woman to death with the Atomic Gauntlet before throwing her body into a man and then shooing both of them with the D.O.O.M. Shooter.

"That means Mallory and Damon were having incest."

"Darwin damn this! Is that seriously what you're worried about right now?" Kronos asked angrily with a laugh. He grabbed a man by the face and activated the current in his gauntlet, peeling the flesh and muscles off of the man before throwing him to the ground. "That's literally the smallest problem here right now. I'm pissed that those bastards carried Mark's body away before I could retrieve my high-tech sunglasses."

"I know that we have bigger problems! I just wanted to tell someone, and you happen to be the closest person nearby. I don't think **The Sinful Son** has realized it yet. I don't think it's full incest, though. Either way, I'm not telling him," Timothy said with a slight laugh as he injected himself with a speed drug and a heart drug. He shook with speed. "It's hero time for real," he yelled before speeding off into the battle like a green lightning bolt, knocking down agents all along his path.

The woman screamed and tried to tear out her hair, prevented from doing so due to the suit. Isabel clung to her screaming mother, and she cried as she watched people get killed in gruesome ways. "Don't worry, sweetie," the woman said to Isabel, her voice shaking. "I know it looks bad, but we can handle this." The truth, however, was that the five men were injuring and killing multiple agents by themselves like humans were powerless insects compared to them. Despite the endless number of agents there, their knives and guns were practically useless against the unique individuals their boss had created. The woman turned to her husband. "Gene, what the fuck is going on here?"

"There's no need to cuss. Relax, dear," Gene commanded coldly. "I knew he would free them, and I wanted that magnetic man to free them. Birch was given that armor for the same reason I allowed that man to free them. I wouldn't expect your soft heart to understand, but in front of my own eyes, before me and happening in real-time, *I wanted* to experience all of their powers before they died," Gene revealed as he watched the five men fighting for their lives in front of him.

"You didn't tell me, and you've endangered our lives and Isabel's life too," the woman complained as she covered Isabel's ears. "How could you allow this to happen? You're jeopardizing our entire operation."

"After decades of hard work, sacrifice, and dedication, I deserve this moment," Gene snapped. "In fact, if they manage to survive, I'll let them escape and live. Now hush!" Gene looked on at the unbelievable battle before him, enthralled by it all and proud of his first major project. To him, the sacrifices taking place and the fighting going on was nothing more than a cinematic masterpiece he had spent years putting together to watch just once.

The Sinful Son, the most aggressive and devastating of the five men, was an unkillable and unstoppable menacing beast as he killed man and woman, one after the other. Encompassed in a dark storm of black smoke and chemicals that destroyed the gut microbiome, he was a true natural disaster. He was worst than a nightmare. He was real. Far more powerful and dangerous than when he had first arrived, storming out of the setting sun, **The Sinful Son** mutilated body after body. He broke bones, smashed human skulls together, choked people, stomped on people, stabbed people with the spikes on his knuckles, ripped out ribs, tore off limbs, and roared to his broken heart's content in his ultimate mission of revenge. Every cell of his natural body was packed with uncontrollable rage, and he used this unholy power to charge through groups of agents, seeming to kill people just by touching them. Small mounds and hills of corpses began to surround the monster as Damon emotionally disintegrated into nothing but an old memory, and **The Sinful Son** took over as the one true lifeform.

No longer holding back, saddened to have to reject his humanity, but knowing that it was necessary to survive, Birch Willow finally lived up to the nickname The Ruthless Root as he swung his giant fists around in a circle, knocking down several agents at a time. He cracked the ground apart with his powerful steps, and he used large clumps of it to blind his enemies. Birch, with superhuman speed and strength, plowed through groups of agents. Repeatedly punching and stomping people, Birch pulverized human bones into gravel and organs into jelly, all with a single blow from his immense attacks. All he needed was a single punch or kick to break multiple bones in a person or cause internal bleeding. He threw people all over the place with unrelenting fury and strength, using their flying bodies to knock down other agents. Picking up four agents, two in each hand, Birch spun around, hitting down several agents. He then used the bodies like twin nightsticks to beat others with. Birch crushed people with his giant feet, caved skulls in, dislocated and tore off limbs, broke every bone imaginable, and ultimately left all crushed after experiencing the might of Charleston Crusher. He even ripped whole bodies in half. His monstrous build was unrivaled.

A manipulator of atoms, the second smartest human to have ever existed, and a user of lethal inventions, **King Kronos** obliterated everyone and anyone that dared to defy him. The D.O.O.M. Shooter was a war's worth of deaths in a single gun, and it's disintegrating beam tore through human bodies like a laser through thin paper as Kronos directed it through entire lines and groups of agents at a time, also sharpshooting and dodging bullets. Blood and guts were spilled everywhere as the beam tore through flesh, nerves, muscles, and bones. Anyone who dared to stray near Kronos was slashed open by his Deconstructor Blade, their life ending there. He stabbed people through the heart, stomach, face, and he sliced several arms and legs off, showing no mercy. He punched and grabbed people with the Atomic Gauntlet, his lethal hand causing a slow and painful death to those now missing large clusters and layers of atoms from their body. Bullets reflected off of the R.N.T. Suit and lab coat as Kronos weaved his way through the crowd, proving that he was the most powerful being alive as he disintegrated everything and everyone into nothing more than drifting atomic particles.

Boosted by additional and purer oxygen, John Leach showed that The Immortalizer was not only invulnerable and immortal but also a veteran and former vigilante as he shot down and killed all who stood in between him and freedom. Continually equipping himself with the guns from fallen agents, John fired a bullet every second, shooting every agent multiple times. He broke arms, legs, and necks as he fought numerous agents at a time, using moves and techniques from every fighting style in the world. He punched, bruised, and kicked, defeating agents slowly but surely. John took the force of agents and their bullets through his suit and used it to destroy their own allies. He stole guns left and right, emptying out full magazines before the agents could even blink. He had sought death for his entire life, and upon arriving at the opportunity, he was turning back, realizing that life was far more valuable. He had found the creators, and he felt that it was Cape Cod Crusader's final mission to destroy them. After that, he was more than willing to go back to Ava and live a good life.

Out of time-grenades but determined to be the first and greatest hero, Timothy used his advanced mind, speed, and strength to defeat anyone in his path. His heart and nerves pulsing faster than ever, he ran like a speeding maniac across the battlefield, helping out his brothers along the way. A bullet of speed and strength, Timothy was almost just a green blur as he darted from spot to spot, knocking out and killing agents as he ran past them at incredible speeds. The Chronological Changer swung the Whip-Watch around in large arcs, slicing people open or smashing them in the head. Those men and woman had just run out of time as Timothy Edward Godwin killed them before they even knew what happened, delivering hundreds of punches in a single minute, or sending people flying back with devastating kicks from his powerful legs. He hit agents with so many high-speed and powerful punches in a single session of seconds that they were a human being one second and then an amorphous blob of bruises, collapsed organs, and broken bones in the next second. He was faster than the agents. He was faster than bullets. He was faster than time itself.

After quickly talking with Birch, whose hardened heart braced itself, Timothy ran after the fleeing woman and Isabel, who were running away from the battle scene, escorted by several agents. Timothy launched the Whip-Watch through the air, wrapping the clock and chain around Isabel's neck before quickly dashing toward Birch, pulling her through the air behind him. He pulled and moved the Whip-Watch in a way that it unwrapped itself from around Isabel, causing her to stumble and spin. As she spun and stumbled in a circle, Birch came soaring through the air with his arms outstretched to either side of him. As he landed, breaking apart the ground, he brought his massive and muscular arms and hands together in a powerful thunderclap that completely flattened Isabel's small skull, killing her instantly.

The woman screamed in despair.

"It is finished," Gene whispered coldly. "All is complete. Time to roll the credits." He quickly commanded a message which was relayed from his advanced phone into the earpiece that every agent wore.

Having received the crucial order, the agents all switched their attention to Birch, who had taken a moment to look at Isabel's seemingly innocent blood, which was smeared all over his willow-themed armored hands. Aiming at his exposed bald head, all of the closest agents fired faster than Birch could dodge or block. Timothy and John were close by but too slow to save him. All of the agents had fired several rounds, and more bullets flew in and out of Birch's skull than bees at a vicious nest on a summer day. Chunks of blood-honey and brain-honeycomb came spewing out. His massive body staggered backward, still alive for a short moment, as the giant reached into the air, utter shock in the remains of his eyes before he fell backward with a heavy thud that shook the ground like an earthquake and echoed across the suddenly quiet fields. His skull had been pulverized by the swarming army of bullets into thousands of small pieces. The small remainders of his flesh were all ripped and torn, stained red, and the mouth he had used to smile at so many people was just a gaping hole filled with biological debris and flooding with blood.

The grotesque death caught everyone's attention. It was so inhumane that Birch's four brothers, although they had just found out that they were related and had only just met him, mourned for the dead giant. Their hearts broke as they looked on at the corpse, whose face was unrecognizable.

Distracted as he was by the unexpected tragedy, Kronos made the grave mistake of allowing the D.O.O.M. Shooter to be ripped from his hands and thrown. The experimental weapon went flying through the air and landed in the controlling hands of Gene. His dark green eyes were shining mercilessly as a severe expression formed on his face. "It's time for me to finish this project," he exclaimed aggressively for everyone to hear. "Now, *die!*" Gene held down the trigger and a beam of unnatural electricity fired from the gun onto John. Tearing through the remaining scraps of his uniform, the beam collided with the suit. The impenetrable suit was, indeed, the ultimate atomic structure, but the D.O.O.M. Shooter was designed to be the ultimate destroyer of atomic structures, second only to antimatter. The suit resisted the current, for the atoms were bonded more tightly than any atoms ever discovered, but the strength of those bonds merely delayed the inevitable. The suit sent rays of it flying all around, killing some agents as it did. The other scientists ducked down, avoiding the vaporizing rays that reflected off of the suit like lights on a disco ball. One refracted beam went across the R.O.M.A.B.A. Industries building, causing it to collapse on itself. The main building of the economical and scientific empire crumbled loudly like a nuclear warhead devestating an entire city.

After a few more seconds of resisting the fatal current, the front of the suit split open, forming a hole that grew bigger, and the current rippled throughout the atomic structure. A large surge of the current flowed upward, and the black mask cracked, cracked some more, and then shattered into pieces. The suit split up and instantly dispersed through the air atomically. A few strands of the suit still clung tightly to John's back and skin, but it was futile. John was no longer The Immortal Man.

Now lacking the suit's regulation system, John was exposed to the cold air, and his entire body grew numb as his capillaries and veins began to grow narrow and close up. The blood flow was restricted to his organs, which were in shock and trying to actually maintain homeostasis for the first time in decades. On top of that, the air he now breathed was not as pure or as light as the filtered air, and he coughed violently, coughing up mucus and blood. He was barely conscious, for his brain was severely lacking oxygen. Yet, as cruel as life would allow it, John was conscious enough to be in excruciating pain. Not only were his insides all failing, but he was being tormented simultaneously by both the cold air that he was not used to as well as the burning exposure to the sun's U.V. rays. Given that the sun had just set and only a few lingering rays remained, the sun's power was almost gone, but John had not been exposed to such U.V. rays in over a century, and his skin blistered and burned. On top of rotting away in an instant, his body being invaded by bacteria far different from that of the 1900s, John was being both frozen and burnt to death at the same time. He could not move. He could not scream. He could barely even think. His whole body convulsed like a small seizure. John's skin shriveled up, his dark eyes bulged, and his dry mouth, which was finally free, was able to utter only one thing as he died. "*Carly*," he called out in a soft whisper. And then, The Immortal Man fell onto his side and was finally dead. A bitter half-smile decorated his decayed face, which only added to the grievous pain the remaining three brothers felt.

Powered by vengeance, justice, and a growing fear inside, the three remaining men were difficult to kill as they fought even more violently than before.

Blending in with the lingering rays of the sunset and sky, which seemed to be ablaze more so than ever before, as if Hell had switched places with Heaven, torrents of vicious flames burst onto the field out of nowhere. Two large agents equipped with flamethrowers had jumped out of one vehicle, and they were headed straight toward *The Sinful Son*. He noticed them immediately, all while still fighting several agents on either side of him. His limbs were a fury of movements, but his torso stood tall and erect, his burning gaze staring at the flames approaching him. The red of his artificial eyes grew brighter and turned into a darker shade of red as if he were summoning unholy power straight from the core of Hell itself. In his dark-infested skull that contained unholy power and monstrous thoughts, *The Sinful Son* remembered through the eerie words and memories what Elder Damon had spoken to him during his nightmarish vision.

With an unholy roar that could have challenged Satan's most barbaric outcry against God, *The Sinful Son* instantly spread his arms out to each side with immense strength, knocking everyone around him to the ground. Still screaming out monstrously through the power of the endless air and wrath within him, shaking the air with his demonic voice, which ominously echoed across the field of death, **The Sinful Son** ran toward the flamethrowers unstoppably. *They thought that they could stop me with one of nature's most savage powers: fire.* Each stomping step of his metal boots flattened the grass and cracked the ground as he dug into the dirt and ran forward as fast as darkness came after light was gone. His black cloak menacingly whipped behind him, and his size seemed to have grown much larger. He still bellowed out like a savage monster as he thundered forward unstoppably. *The wicked blaze raged like the anger and hate in my heart like the molten magma of a volcano beneath the Earth upon its core, but it was no match for me.* The two agents stayed steady in their approach towards the monstrous being charging at them, although they seemed to grow more nervous with each second that passed. *It is true that I escaped barely alive, but* **The Sinful Son** *will always survive.* **The Sinful Son**, turned so that only his backside would catch the flames, and the agents were forced to stop the fires in order to avoid hitting each other.

Using this moment to his advantage, **The Sinful Son** swiftly killed the two flamethrower-welding agents, letting loose another roar of unstoppable power before he ran over to the tallest pile of corpses he had made and stood on top of it. Due to the flames, **The Sinful Son** threw off his unholy garments and exosuit, revealing his human form, which was far more powerful and unstoppable as he broke free of his restraints. The agents hesitated and gasped, shocked by the unholy sight of immense power and intimidation, simultaneously attracted by his perfect looks and repelled by the monstrous marks of his past. Before a single agent could fire a gun or charge forward, **The Sinful Son** stopped roaring monstrously, and the entire field of death grew quiet. An unspoken truce was made between Timothy, Kronos, and the remaining agents as they all stopped and looked on at the divine and unholy scene of **The Sinful Son**. His entire body tense and shaking, he froze in place for a brief moment before falling to one knee and trying to stand, resisting his inevitable death. The unholy power of ***The Sinful Son*** now too much for Damon's mortal body to handle, he collapsed and died upon the mound of corpses from internal complications caused by his raging blood.

Timothy served as a human buzzsaw as he spun his Whip-Watch at superhuman speeds. It had been specifically designed to withstand high-speed impacts. Running around almost faster than they eye could see at such a close range, Timothy burst past Gene, using the Whip-Watch to knock the D.O.O.M. Shooter out of his true father's hands. It fell to the ground and was kicked around by all the commotion of the agents. He stopped running and faced Gene.

It was just Timothy and Gene in a wide space, and Gene raised his hand to stop several agents from coming over to help him. The battle was solely a duel now.

Gene slowly chuckled as he stared into the scratched steampunk goggles, which reflected his own image back at him. "What brings you here, young Timothy? Come to be the hero and defeat the final villain on your first journey? Has seeing the death of your brothers pushed you past all of your limits?" Without warning, Timothy sprinted past Gene in a green blur and stopped a few feet behind him. Gene slowly turned around, chuckling proudly. "Trying to intimidate me? Your speed is truly impressive, but is it wise of you to abandon Kronos when three of your brothers have already been killed?"

"You and I both know that he's more than capable of handling himself," Timothy replied firmly, his emotions unreadable. He had a full mustache now and the beginning of a beard. A majority of his hair was dark grey. "I've come to stop your evil. After everything that's happened, I've come to believe your crazy story of the past and the truth of our presents. You still haven't explained how you got our fake parents to raise us. Did you pay them, have them adopt us, or did you switch us at birth? I bet you switched us with similar babies and parents who slightly matched our physical appearance and then took their baby and made them into an agent! I still don't understand what your goals are or were. Why are you doing all of this? None of that matters, though. After hearing some of the things you manipulated in the lives of my brothers, there's no doubt in my mind that *you* did it… but I want to hear you admit it."

"Of course, I understand. I always did, and I always will. You want to hear me say it? How noble of you, or perhaps selfish as you all are. I'll say it, though, Timothy, since you can't kill me, and I have no guilt for what happened. I admit that I, G.O.D., killed your father to force you into a life with just your vile mother and to further push you toward heroism so that you would become the man you are today," Gene yelled despicably at Timothy. "I also made sure that you won the lottery so you would have the necessary money to get the resources you needed! Does that make you happy?"

Timothy burst forward like a bullet, hitting Gene with a barrage of dozens of punches per second at superhuman speeds. His movements were untrackable. One fist smashed Gene over and over again with sorrow, while the other fist smashed him over and over again with rage. Timothy hit the immovable concrete-man like two jackhammers at full speed and power. When he stopped punching and jumped back, Timothy was shocked to see Gene standing firm, the grasses below him flattened, and the dirt cracked. In fact, Gene was standing in a hole a few feet deep.

"If I wanted to, I could have pressed my hand against you and allowed you to have been hit with the force of your own punches in your torso, which is already a bit injured from your fight this morning. That probably would have killed you. I'm merciful, though. I *can* be killed. You just have to be willing to kidnap me and then keep me hostage until you manage to do so." Timothy took a step forward, but Gene raised his hand. "However, as cliche as it is, I'm afraid you'll have to choose between doing that or helping him," Gene stated cockily as he pointed past Timothy at Kronos.

Still killing as many agents as he could and surviving, Kronos was fighting with his Deconstructor Blade and Atomic Gauntlet, but he was getting more outnumbered with each passing second. It was just him against an army that Gene had been building for decades. Not completely bulletproof all over his entire body, Kronos was having a hard time defending and dodging while fighting off his attackers. He saw Timothy and Gene, instantly understanding what was going on. "Don't let him escape! I'll be fine on my own," Kronos stated as he fell to one knee, fighting off three agents at once.

Timothy used all the speed and heart drugs he had left, stacking them on top of each other, and exceeding the limits his body could handle. His mind had never been thinking so fast. His body moved at incredible speeds. In a green blur, he ran over and defeated the many agents surrounding Kronos, but more were coming. He helped his brother onto his feet. "I wasn't going to leave you to die. You're my friend and my brother."

Kronos watched in utter horror as Timothy's skin wrinkled, his hair turned grey, his veins showed more, as he lost weight, and as he slowly grew shorter. "You're pushing yourself too hard! Just leave me and help yourself! Capture that bastard and find a way to kill him. Go to my castle and find the Atomic Chainsaw to cut through his suit or search for the D.O.O.M. Shooter. At this rate, you'll die," Kronos stated gravely.

"I know," Timothy replied in a deep and raspy voice. "I'm aware of that, and I'm okay with it. You have a better chance of defeating Gene than I do." He ran in a circle, pummeling through the new wave of agents, and then the wave beyond that before returning back to Kronos. "It's written in the Bible and in every comic lore that there is no greater thing a person can do than to sacrifice themselves or to lay down their lives for others." He grabbed Kronos and ran to a new spot as several bullets went ripping through the air at the two men. "Kronos... I forgive you, and I hope that you'll forgive me. We don't need a hero to defeat that villain, but we need an even greater villain." Timothy's voice grew raspier as his hair began to turn white, a full beard hanging from his face. "This is my final act as a hero and the redeeming choice that will allow me to rest peacefully." He quickly ran another circle around the lone survivor, using the Whip-Watch to knock down several charging agents. "I'm almost out of time, but I still have enough time to do one last thing!" Timothy exclaimed as he charged at Kronos, grabbing his thumb and forcing it onto the finger-lock, activating the R.N.T. Suit. "Kronos, *gooooooo*," the white-haired and weak Timothy yelled. As Kronos began to deconstruct into atoms before being teleported away, he looked at Timothy, whose fearful face managed to cry a few tears before collapsing to the ground, a dead skin-clothed skeleton with overgrown hair.

In an invisible flash of light and atomic particles, Kronos was gone in just an instant. The field of death miles away, Kronos was reconstructed at the castle library, and he collapsed to the floor. His eyes flickered open and shut as he looked up at the painting of the ocean, the exact one he had looked at before he left for his journey, with fuzzy eyes. He stretched his arm out in an attempt to reach it, but he was too weak. As his brain cells were consumed by his own immune system and his body slowly shut down, Kronos' delirious mind was healthy enough to let out a final tear goodbye. He did not want to die. Not alone. Not like this. As the last of his brain was destroyed, Kronos passed away, alone and afraid. His parents had won. The Genetic Corporation was victorious.

REVIEW AND RESULTS

(Somewhere in North America. A Few Days Later. 2022)

Gene sat waiting in his temporary office, the walls blocking the sound of construction as the new main building for The Genetic Corporation was being built around him. The room was small and white, the walls lined with tape for painting. In the center of the room, there was one desk and a rolly chair. The desk had a single high-tech computer on it, and a fancy wooden plaque with gold that read "G.O.D." across the golden front.

The only door to the room, which was across from the front of the desk, began to creak as it slowly began to open, the individual causing the action hidden and hesitant. Gene was twirling a ballpoint pen around in his right hand. Pushing the chair back just a micrometer, he looked up as Abraham entered the room, his left leg now a standard artificial one until a team of agents finished crafting one for him unlike any other. There had been too many bullets in his leg to keep it on him, and so they had been forced to cut it off. Abraham hobbled forward nervously, using a cane to help support him. Even so, he could not help but tremble all over. He bowed slightly.

Gene pulled out his white pocket watch, the case encrusted with a green D.N.A. strip diagonal across it, and he checked the time. He closed the watch with a disapproving growl in his throat, his face appearing hardened and dry as if it had been out in the sun for several days despite the mask. "You're late for our meeting, Dr. Abraham. That is very unlike you, and it reflects poorly on The Genetic Corporation."

"My sincerest apologies, G.O.D. I was unable to witness the final moments of the operation's success due to my injury, but I was informed that afterward, you and your wife disappeared and have been silent and absent except for your call this morning, which was to me only."

"That is correct. My wife is mourning, no doubt, and I have been doing work that is vital for the future. Overseeing the combination of my creations' scientific breakthroughs into one unstoppable force is not a task that I would entrust to anyone other than myself. Besides that, I've also been preparing everything for The Genetic Corporation to go public and announce that we have officially taken over R.O.M.A.B.A. Industries after purchasing it. At least, that's what the world will know, anyway."

Abraham dropped to his one healthy knee and hung his head down. "It is because of my carelessness and failure to predict and account variables that Isabell was killed. Though I did not witness it for myself, several agents described the brutal death to me. She should not have been so gruesomely murder like that! The blame can easily be placed upon me, and it was in no way your fault, as you do not make mistakes. Therefore, I am willing to accept any punishment you see fit t-"

His dark green eyes looking down on Abraham, Gene raised his hand in a sign to stop. "I am undoubtedly the most powerful and most intelligent person to have ever existed and to ever exist, but you do not need to humble and downgrade yourself so much, as long as you maintain respect and fear. Secondly, do not assign blame to anyone, including yourself, Abraham. I'll inform you, and *only* you, that Isabell's death was already planned and accounted for on my part. So, do not even think about it again. While it may seem awful of me to know that my only true daughter would die and I did nothing to stop it, the truth is that Isabell's death was necessary for the future."

"As expected of you, G.O.D. However, a being such as myself fails to see how her death has benefitted anyone or will benefit our company at all," Abraham said humbly as he stood up.

"My wife is too kind and morally-conflicted, is she not?"

Abraham hesitated, but he trusted Gene and knew him to be a reasonable and honest man. "Unfortunately, sir, I'm afraid that, with all due respect, your wife is not as willing to make the hard choices and sacrifices that you have always made and continue to make for the sake of all humanity. Her softness is part of what almost prevented and then later almost ruined our operation with the scientists. Of course, mothers tend to have a special bond with their children, regardless of how they're created and-"

"That's enough. You certainly worded that perfectly to spare yourself from my wrath, but I assure you that I am aware of my wife's flaws. Except for myself, all humans have flaws. I shall fix that, of course, but more importantly, do you understand that point that I'm trying to make regarding Isabell's death?"

"As cruel as it is, I do understand, and I thank you for setting me up to understand what your plan entailed regarding that matter. It was in the best interest of our company and the future, so I accept what happened and shall not dwell upon it any longer. You allowed your wife to grow close to Isabell, knowing that Isabell was going to be killed during the operation. Through the death of her only true daughter at the hands of the scientific sons she hoped to spare, your wife has grown colder and bitter, to say the least. At the same time, her hatred for anyone who stands against us or anyone who will try to oppose The Genetic Corporation has drastically increased. In conclusion, she's become more capable of making the hard decisions and sacrifices that you do, which is vital for our survival and plans."

"That's entirely correct, Abraham. You've impressed me with your comprehension of vague details and predictable variables, and I praise you for your answer. It would seem that this whole operation with the scientists has greatly improved your ability to think, and your importance to the company only increases with each passing day."

"You are far too kind!" Abraham bowed. "Please understand that I am not worthy of such praise, G.O.D. You waste your breath and valuable thoughts praising my intellect, and it is only because of your guidance and incomprehensible levels of endless genius beyond humanity that I have managed to become as smart as I am now."

"You can stop bowing. Raise your head. You deserved a bit of praise considering all that you've done for The Genetic Corporation during your years of service here. Enjoy the moment. Unfortunately, the rest of the conversation is going to be rather unpleasant. There are a lot of rumors circulating around our company these past few days, and I've heard quite a lot. You've done your best to try and fix the mistakes that were made during that operation, which is completely understandable, and I appreciate the effort, but you've failed in that regard, Abraham."

"Please, I-"

"However, I shall not punish you as of now, since it would be unfair to do so before absolutely knowing everything that happened and is currently happening consequently. Understand that I'm not angry, and, as a man of my word, I promise that I'm not and will not be angry. Most of the rumors I've heard would suggest that everything was beyond your knowledge or control. As of right now, I simply wish to know what happened."

"My apologies, sir. The inconvenience is nothing that you should have your time wasted by, as you have more pressing matters to deal with, but I shall rightfully inform you of everything going on, as the dominoes are creating a bigger effect than I had anticipated. Unfortunately, what you've heard and spoken is true, as always. There was a major problem, which has rippled throughout the water of our company and plans, creating several disturbances."

"I figured that was the case, and I'm utterly displeased to know, but I shall not blame anyone just yet. Explain it all to me."

"Of course. I truly hate to be the one to tell you this, but after you left with your wife, we experienced some… difficulties."

"Difficulties? Were all the scientists not killed?"

"That part must be explained later. There's a bigger problem before that. Your prodigy, Kronos, was several steps ahead as always. I'm afraid we didn't account for that."

"Are you accusing me of not accounting for every variable?" Gene asked with a threatening glare in his eye, which meant death for whoever was caught in its gaze.

"No, sir! As a loyal subordinate of yours, I know that nothing is beyond your comprehension or intellectual abilities. I'm saying that Kronos is more like you than you had perhaps realized due to your lack of a direct relationship with him. He was planning just as you were, as a result of your godly genes, sir. The casualties were honorable sacrifices as always, but many more died than planned, and that's on top of the interference from the magnetic figure and… *The Sinful Son*," Abraham said with anger over his leg.

"I see," Gene said emotionlessly as he twirled the pen in and out of his fingers, his gaze now on the surface of the desk as he thought over everything. "Understand that I knew the magnetic individual was going to come, and I was impressed by his science and technology. The fact that he did not stay and fight is rather puzzling. Is he a coward, a man without care, or was he staying back to fight another day? We'll have to try and monitor him if we can. I'm still trying to figure him out for the future. We know he's a bit reckless and kind of a punk, but he's also good-natured and gentleman-like at other times. It might be that he has bi-polar disorder or dissociative identity disorder, which makes him a lot more difficult to control or manipulate." Gene shook his head. "Never mind that, however, as that can be discussed a different day. Regarding the issues created by my brilliant creation Kronos, what happened?"

"In a way, I suppose we can assume that he had a backup plan."

"A backup plan?"

"Yes. He had the R.N.T. Suit edited to work in conjunction with other creations wirelessly upon activation. The servants had not picked up on this."

"Those two were specifically chosen by me for their high intellects and observational abilities, as well as their training in infiltration and the field of spying. Did they not read over all of his blueprints, computer files, and even test the R.N.T. Suit out? Everything that technology was capable of should have been in our knowledge."

"Exactly as you say it is, sir. The outcome is a result of something that went unobserved, placing the time of editing within the past few days, which is long after he was in contact with the servants."

"Hmm. Understand that the servants were not always at his side or within the range of being able to hear him. So, he could have done it at any time, really. Kronos was a hard man to spy on, which is why we had to use real people to get close to him in the first place. If he was even the slightest bit suspicious of the servants, however, he probably waited until he was on his journey. It would be the perfect time to make a move against us for the future that he suspected was coming."

"You've figured it out as always, sir, but permission to point out a flaw in that plan without punishment?"

"Permission granted, Abraham. What's wrong with that theory?"

"We were watching him constantly, or we at least knew what he was doing and where he was. At least ever since he left the castle. Given the fact that most of the past few days were spent on the road for him, or in the company of the other scientists, how could Kronos have possibly edited the R.N.T. Suit without the proper resources to do so or the amount of time required for such a contingency ability?"

"A fair point, but I'm afraid that your mind is too simplistic in situations like this. I've already figured out two possible events in which he had the resources and time to do so. Three, actually."

"My apologies, sir," Abraham said while hanging his head in shame. "Please forgive me for being unable to grasp the possibilities that are easily understandable."

"There's no need," Gene said with a dismissive gesture of his hand. "Please, raise your head. This is a plan that has spanned for many decades. Over a century, in fact. You understand more of our plan and the company than anybody else in The Genetic Corporation, and I value your intelligence."

"I am unworthy of such praise, sir, but I thank you for it. I humbly ask that you help me understand what I have failed to figure out."

"The night of Birch Willow's presentation, we had two agents at the gym. They were there to keep an eye on Sir Thomas, Birch Willow, and Michael Kellson. Kronos, however, was not at the presentation. He was out in his custom car. The problem with Kronos is that he instinctively destroys all cameras within his location using the D.O.O.M. Shooter, making it rather difficult to keep an eye on him. That's besides the fact that he uses jammers and custom-internets and other ways of making himself non-existent, but I'm sure you understand the simple point I'm trying to make. While we knew that his car was parked in the alleyway, we could not actually see him. Given how advanced the car was, it's quite possible that he was inside it working on the R.N.T. Suit while no one was around."

"I understand, sir, but are you suggesting that he had stashed the tools and equipment necessary in the trunk ahead of time? In that case, we greatly underestimated his intellect and ability to plan ahead. Such an idea is pure genius!"

"It is. However, an even smarter idea, as well as a more logical one, is that he worked on the R.N.T. Suit at the island that Mallory Leach owned. Dodging the camera systems there, as well as the audio-recording devices, he would have had all of the resources he needed, as well as a calm environment to work."

"Your intellect is far beyond human comprehension, sir. I believe that sounds like the most plausible theory. However, it's important for the reputation of The Genetic Corporation that the two servants be talked to by you, if not punished."

"I see. I'll take care of those two later."

"Well, sir, there's actually something you should know about the servants and, specifically, Agent Elizabeth."

"In a moment, Abraham," Gene snapped back harshly as he raised his hand in a gesture to stop. "I already know about the issues with her and Kronos, and they're not important right now. First, I must know about what he changed in the R.N.T. Suit to activate this backup plan of his. It is top priority information."

"Of course, sir. My apologies. Allow me to explain what happened. I suppose Kronos knew that if he were to ever teleport again, it would only be in the most desperate of situations, and perhaps even that it would not be on his own terms. Accounting for this, he set the suit to correspond to a failsafe. When he teleported, it activated a series of bombs that he had buried underneath the R.O.M.A.B.A. Industries store."

Gene's eyes grew harsher than they naturally were, and all of the ice in the Arctic could not have matched the severe cold that now filled their darkness. His chest swelled, and every fiber of muscle in his body tensed up at once. "What did you just say? Now, I actually am extremely aggravated because his research was the most important."

"He blew up all of R.O.M.A.B.A. Industries, sir, but the nuclear weapon he had cached was not activated, for some reason. We are still looking into that, or we're going to, as soon as we can. We are unsure as to whether or not its failure to detonate was intentional on his part to scare us or something."

"You better look into it! I want us there before anyone else! Even in the remote locations at which that building is stationed, there are bound to be media companies heading over there soon. Even government officials and the local enforcement agencies might head over there. That will jeopardize a lot of our operation. That aggravates me. The store wasn't our main target, but taking over it and stealing all of the advanced products in it was a bonus worth a lot."

"We will do beyond our best, sir. The difficulties don't end there, however. The store, I'm afraid, was the smallest casualty. The R.N.T.

Suit also activated a series of bombs in the two laboratories, destroying the teleportation machines. Then a nuclear-like weapon, a scale of four acres, went off at the castle, and we assume the source to be either a bomb in the castle or the inner workings of the R.N.T. Suit in addition to atomic manipulation through the use of the current. We've essentially lost all of his research, sir. All we have now is the D.O.O.M. Shooter."

"Hmph," Gene replied deeply within the base of his throat. He tapped the pen against the desk almost faster than the human eye could see, his dark gaze unreadable yet still overwhelmingly powerful. "That is unacceptable, and I require more research on such an event. I never foresaw such a catastrophe, and that's impossible. How could the planting of so many explosive devices go undetected by all of us? Such a chain of events means that Benjamin failed to detect and observe as he was supposed to. I personally trained him. How utterly disappointing. Kill him."

"Right away, G.O.D. He should be tortured and severely punished first for costing us almost everything we worked hard to get."

"However, let's not forget about Kronos' unique vehicle and everything secretly stored within it, Abraham. Everything in that vehicle is just as critical to us as everything we just lost, and it does make up for the heavy losses we've suffered."

"I've accounted for that, sir," Abraham said nervously. He took a micro-step backward. "The car automatically sped off to some unknown location, and we were unable to track it. More importantly, sir, you should know that the vehicle took Laura Godwin and Spencer Edward Godwin with it."

"Is he trying to build a team for the future, or is he merely saving the lives of his allies' loved ones?"

"I am not capable of answering such a question, G.O.D. You are the only one who can figure it out. Either way, Kronos planned everything out so that nothing in his life could be taken, and we assume the car and what's contained in it were sent to someone or are for some future plan that he crafted ahead of time. There is also another problem regarding Kronos. The vehicle is out there somewhere, but so is a large portion of his research, we believe. Benjamin and Mark did report two things that connect and-”

“That bastard!” Gene nodded his head. “He got rid of the research that we could access and moved everything else away so that we could not get it, but that leaves the question of who he’s saving it for. He is long dead, but his plans live on for the next few years to come. Kronos and I are two intellectual geniuses who will continue to rival each other, and he acted unsure just to trick us even more.” Gene smirked, and all life nearby seemed to freeze. “I’m looking forward to it.”

Using all of his energy, Abraham managed not to faint. “Why would you be looking forward to it, sir? Are you referring to one of the reasons you made the scientists?”

“This project and operation were always meant to be messy and a bit unpredictable. Being the smartest person to have ever existed and to ever exist has made me bored. Through the creation of the scientists, I was able to have fun, because the scale of variables and manipulation was larger than anyone has ever tried to understand and play with before.”

“Ah, I understand,” Abraham said with a bow. “Forgive me for my ignorance and failure to understand. It is only natural that you would be the only one able to master and even be capable of such a large-scale project. I am very humbled and honored to have been your direct subordinate these past few years for this project, and I look forward to the future you have planned for The Genetic Corporation and the world.”

“That’s correct, so tell me everything that went wrong, because, for the first time since my intelligence first manifested, I’m actually starting to worry a bit, and it’s quite enjoyable to experience this feeling of competition. Of course, I know I’ll always win, but it’s still an opponent worthy enough to scratch me if they attack hard enough, and that pain is something I’ve never felt.” Gene looked at Abraham. “What’s wrong? Your knees won’t stop quivering, you’re sweating and gulping, and all life is drained from every cell in your body. There's no need to fear my unfathomable power, Abraham. I am your rightful leader who serves justly."

"Of course. I'll continue with the reports. See, Mark was always bitter over the lightning incident, but none of us could have predicted that, and the consequence was purely an aesthetic and personal one regarding him. However, that led to a greater hatred for Kronos to exist in his heart, and that resulted in their confrontation during the final phase of the operation. While this did not actually impact anything significantly, it did end up with Mark getting himself killed. His efforts weren't in vain, however, as he was able to send out an audio message to me. That's what he was doing with his phone before he died. His message was simple, but the meaning behind it could be devastating to us in a way that completely destroys the company!"

"No exaggeration?"

"Sir, if what Mark said is true, the world will undoubtedly turn against The Genetic Corporation and destroy us. He may have died, but his message is actually what will save us because only he realized the inevitable threat that awaits us all!"

Believing Abraham and menacingly chuckling on the inside just a bit, Gene grew even more severe while smirking, the mischievous grin sinister in its malicious entertainment. "The stakes are quite high then, and that makes it all the more interesting. Kronos is proving to be a lot smarter and more challenging than I thought, but it only proves how much of a genius I am, and while I'm not egotistic like he was, I do enjoy the praise and truth. I don't think you're lying or exaggerating, as you've always been an honest and reliable man, Abraham, so I'll trust that we're all in grave danger. Fortunately, my power is enough to entirely eradicate any threat. What was the message?"

"He merely whispered that Kronos' eyes were amber-yellow, and that was it. Most would not be able to understand the message or even think anything of it. However, we all know that all of your children had either brown or green eyes, so that means-"

Gene laughed heartily with pride and joy as he slammed his one fist against the table. "He is truly remarkable! That clever bastard! If only I had been able to have him as a real son. What a brilliant plan of blackmailing us in the future. The color of his eyes indicates contact lenses of the most advanced kind. To improve his skills and abilities, they were most likely designed to enhance his vision with the ability to zoom-in or zoom-out. More importantly, knowing him, they were recording everything. His whole life, ever since he started wearing them, perhaps, has been recorded and saved."

"That's exactly what I fear, G.O.D."

"Either way, just the footage from the operation alone would jeopardize The Genetic Corporation's reputation and future. After all, he would have recorded everything we said, assuming he had a way of recording sound besides just everything he saw. I understand why you are so concerned about it. Not only that, but he made them have a unique color so we would *know* that he has the footage, regardless of whether there is audio or not. He *wanted* us to know that he has it because it's his way of warning and threatening us from beyond death. His genius is immortal, and his legacy will destroy us," Gene said, laughing and proudly impressed.

"Impossible! You believe he knew we were coming? Was this all just a suicide mission? Perhaps not just for him, but he ended all of their lives on purpose?"

"I don't know," Gene replied gruffly, smirking as he turned his gaze to the computer screen, which had the words "NO SIGNAL" in the center. Abraham felt a surge of fear swell within his person, although he tried to keep his throat steady. He had never heard those words come from the mouth of Gene, nor had he ever thought he would. "All I know is that you're right, Abraham. He's more like me than I had imagined him to be, and I like it. He was always the silent type. Despite his yelling and arguing, he always kept the truth to himself, and he always twisted his words to fool other people and me. It's possible that he was combating us the whole time by playing along to give the ultimate blow in the end, but I cannot speak for him or the past. I cannot predict or know the secret plans of a man who is almost as smart as I am. All I can do is predict and simulate, but that's as close as well get, at least for now. When the pieces start coming together, we'll know more, but it's too early for that. He acted like he had accidentally played right into our hands by getting all of the scientists together, but perhaps that was his Trojan Horse after all."

"Of course. I understand, and I shall not think about it or worry unless commanded to. I have no doubt that you'll be able to stop him and save us all, G.O.D."

"Either way, we shall continue on, although it will be challenging to fix everything. While we may have lost almost all of his research, we still managed to get the D.O.O.M. Shooter. That is the most important piece of history and the future, so we can at least celebrate that. We also have his high-tech shades. What about the report from Benjamin? You said it connected with the message that Mark sent."

"After hearing the message from Mark through me, Benjamin pleaded for his life, apologizing for his failure to notice that Kronos' eyes were the wrong color. However, between his shameful and pitful begging, he was able to give me two possible answers regarding where the footage might be located."

Gene perked up in his seat. "Is that so? How *splendid.* That makes all of this easier to clean up, and there's no need to worry at all. We'll simply send a team to each of those locations and retrieve the footage. We cannot destroy it at any cost, because while it has blackmail on us, it might also have enough footage for us to recreate teleportation, the ability to manipulate atoms, and everything else that Kronos ever created."

"My gravest apologies, sir, but we do not actually have two specific locations, which makes what you wish to do more difficult than you believe it will be. Benjamin said that if Kronos were to have recorded everything or to have sent any of his research anywhere, he would either send it to Arctic Asshole or Drunk Diver, if not both."

"Why do I not know who those two individuals are?" Gene asked through clenched teeth behind the mask as he powerfully slammed his fist against the table.

"I suppose he thought those two individuals, who he believes might not even be real, to be unimportant and irrelevant information that would have only wasted your time, G.O.D."

"Benjamin was to report everything to me, regardless of whether or not he deemed the information important," Gene bellowed, his condemning voice echoing throughout the barren room and seeming to travel throughout the whole building. "All agents are to follow that order because only I am the one to decide what is important or not important for this company and my work!" Gene yelled as he smashed his fist on the table. "Is that understood? Now, I'm going to have a big meeting with everyone who works for us, and we're going to establish new rules for the future." Gene took a deep breath. "How impudent. Now, tell me about these two individuals."

"The names are just what Benjamin heard Kronos calling the individuals, and his relationship to them is unclear. We know that the man Kronos calls Arctic Asshole is an older gentleman working in Antarctica alone on something huge. Benjamin believes that Arctic Asshole was working on ways to improve humans' ability to live in colder climates and that the man moved to Antarctica, fearing the next war would destroy most liveable countries. Drunk Diver is also an older gentleman, and he is a former sea captain who is doing research on exploring the deepest depths of the ocean and the possibility of building an underwater city or base. Both of the individuals are intelligent and possibly have a scientific breakthrough of their own, but Benjamin only heard the names spoken a few times, and Kronos was vague about his relationship with them and his work. However, those two individuals are the only ones we have right now that are possible locations where Kronos' work might have been sent to, so I will have teams look into those two individuals as soon as possible. After all, who else could it be for?"

"Hmph. Interesting. We only created seven advanced-individuals, yet the total count far surpasses that, and it continues to grow. I can't help but wonder if our work had a rippling effect throughout society, which caused others to seek power and knowledge. Forget that, however, as we'll soon control everything, and it won't matter how many of these self-made heroes, villains, and geniuses exist. How many agents did we lose due to the bombs?"

"I'm afraid too many to count, sir."

"Unfortunate, but we'll have a special funeral procession for all of the agents who died honorable deaths for our company and the future to come. Disregarding Kronos and his work, was everything else secured as planned?" Abraham, who was terrified, hesitated too long. "I asked if everything was secured," Gene yelled as he smashed his fist against the table again, his voice now staying louder than before. "My patience and calmness have already surpassed their limits today, and I've remained reasonable for this whole conversation, but I will not tolerate hesitation. It's clear that a few unpredictable variables threw our plans off rails, but did you manage to secure the other items and research? That was one of the main reasons why this operation was created!"

"The answer is mixed results, sir," Abraham spat out as quickly as he could. "We weren't expecting to lose more than twenty agents at the most when we captured the scientists since they weren't supposed to escape the metal bar, and we ended up losing more than I could count on all of my toes and fingers in addition to each vertebra in my spine. Then the building blew up and killed over fifty agents who were there to secure the scene, and then we lost over a dozen at each laboratory."

Gene sighed powerfully enough to blow Abraham away, had the mask not contained his raging breath. "What did you manage to cover? As the third most powerful person in our company and second-in-charge of all our agents after me, I trust that you were able to work under such harsh conditions as you were trained to."

"I tried my best, sir."

"I know you did, but we'll see the results. Now I have to replan the whole future of the world," Gene bellowed as his chest heaved upward before settling back down. "Do you think that's easy?"

"Not at all. I could never grasp or imagine the responsibilities you have, let alone how much work and difficulty you have to deal with."

"That's correct," Gene stated coldly, his eyes narrowed with contempt. "At this rate, I suppose I'll have to be informed about each scientist individually. Update me on The Immortalizer, then. Don't hesitate or be nervous. I already know it's bad news. I always know. In the name of The Genetic Corporation, I swear that no harsh punishment shall befall you for what you say, as I know it was an outside variable beyond your control."

Abraham could not prevent himself from gulping in terror. He let a small breath of courage rise in his chest. Gene was always correct, but more importantly, he was a man of his word. "If you say so, then I shall continue on with no fear. We were unable to secure the second copy of the suit and mask."

"Hmph. Who has it?"

"The answer to that question is singled out to the two people with whom John Leach shared the existence of the technology. Steven, the middle-aged family man, who has shown to be secretly selfish, and then-"

"Avalyn."

"That *is* the other person, sir. I was getting to her."

"I know she's the other person, and I'm letting you know that she has already equipped the suit and mask for herself, and she defeated the agents sent to retrieve the items. That's why they haven't reported back. Not to mention, she has no problem with the idea of murder. It's been a few days, and she most likely accepted that John leach was never returning to Cape Cod, because he was unable to survive. Upon seeing her, Steven and Avalyn either fought or he left her alone."

"Are you sure?"

"Despite the difficulties as of late, which are presumably not my fault as shall be revealed by the research of our agents, I am *always* sure.

I can tell by a feeling besides the clues and how everything is set up to lead to such a conclusion."

"Then, I suppose The Immortalizer is now a woman."

"That's correct, and there's nothing wrong with that at all. Know that she is just a girl, though, Abraham She is still young and she is haunted by her past and even her present as she now wonders what truly happened to The Immortal Man whom she so admired."

"Understood. Is she a threat to us, sir?"

"Time will tell, although anyone in possession of what she now wears is indeed a threat to all. She also probably knows about our existence, considering that John's life story included him breaking into one of our buildings back in the day When we announce ourselves to the public, as planned, she will most likely recognize us. Especially if she goes through his box of papers and sees our research on telomerase. She might actually seek us out for help, but I already know that she views us as an enemy."

"I suppose that all makes sense. Then we should stop her and retrieve the suit before it's too late! I'll send out a team rig-"

"The Immortalizer has been reborn. We cannot stop her now."

"With all due respect, sir, the suit has one weakness, and we own the machine that takes advantage of that! I see no problem at all with eliminating her if we must."

"We cannot simply kill. She is now a part of our plans for the future, and the D.O.O.M. Shooter will be gone for a while as we use it to combine all of the research we have. Secondly, I'm interested in seeing what kind of person she becomes with that suit and mask."

"Understood. On the bright side, her ex-boyfriend Aaron is perfectly set up and already on his way to becoming a greasy politician who advocates for anti-vigilantism due to his encounter with John."

"That *is* good news, but even with such political power, he will never combat what is to come his way."

"I'm afraid I don't quite understand, and I hope that you might elaborate on that remark."

"I shall reveal to you the unknown then, as I have foreseen what is to come. The identity of **The Sinful Son** is being passed on, just as the gear of The Immortalizer has been passed on. In fact, it has already been passed on. The girl that Damon saved will form a cult of worshippers as she becomes the new representative of the broken."

"Why not stop her now?"

"Stopping a problem a decade or more before it ever happens would give The Genetic Corporation no credit for it, now would it?"

"My apologies for my failure to see such an apparent downfall for the company. I understand now. Still, how will that relate to Aaron?

"As he rises in political power and favor with those who advocate for anti-vigilantism, she shall form a national party that supports vigilantes. Her side will also be backed by those saved by Timothy during his time as a hero, as well as those who have been saved by the magnetic figure. Not to mention the fact that they'll probably have Ava's support. So, as you can see, the political side in favor of heroes is far greater than Aaron, although he will be backed by a lot of citizen and politicians as well. It will tear the country apart until we step in. I will explain the exact details concerning both of those individuals later. As of right now, I must know *everything* that has taken place, given the unforeseen circumstances."

"Of course, G.O.D. However, what I'm about to say might be an even worse problem."

"Intriguing," Gene said with a smirk, inviting the challenge. "What could you possibly have to report?"

"The body of Damon Willow was not recovered, sir. Whether it was the cover of the bombs or something else, his body disappeared. I'm no scientist or genius, but I do know that we never ensured his death by killing him after he had died by his own body. So, there's the possibility that he escaped and is alive."

"How intriguing. To think that no one would attack him just because they thought he was truly dead… yet I don't blame them. Don't worry so much about it, Abraham. There *is* a chance that he survived, whether he was stricken down by a stroke or a brain aneurism. Either way, he most likely wouldn't be the same after such a medical incident. He's no longer **The Sinful Son**, whether he's out there still or not. Will he come into play in the future? Possibly, but I think that if he did survive, he's taking a backseat in life now. What about the man that Mallory Leach let go during one of her countless mental breakdowns?"

"He's already on his way to becoming a major leader of psychology, sir. Despite all that has gone wrong, I assure you that we will help him on that path and be there to recruit him to our side. There's no doubt that he'll be a prominent member of The Genetic Corporation."

"Excellent. He's a stepping stone in the path of the future. What about her child?"

"That foul creature was ripped out of her dead guts, sir. Our agents were on standby and tried to save the child as soon as it was safe and possible to do so. We have the greatest minds in the world, as well as an excellent team of geneticists and doctors trying to preserve the child's life as we speak, although it is very difficult."

"Understood. It doesn't really matter either way. That creature will be viler than Mallory or Damon, though. Therefore, if that thing lives, notify me immediately. What's the status update on Michael Kellson?"

"In the laboratory, sir. They're stripping his D.N.A. as we speak in preparation for what will be done with him."

"Good. What about that kid that Birch mentored?"

"On his way to becoming the future Birch Willow, just minus all of his muscles and cellulase digesting functions."

"Did you take everything from the farm and house?"

"Yes, sir."

"Not all is lost. We have still gained a lot."

"True."

"Stella Godwin?"

"Dies in a car accident tomorrow?"

"Excellent. Mallory's island?"

"A new base is being set up there for our use."

"Good. The magnetic figure?"

"No clue, sir."

"The exosuit and vantablack cloak?"

"Recovered and being repaired."

"Timothy's house?"

"Being investigated. We managed to get some of the syringes from the battle field. All traces of the chemicals in his system were gone by the time we got to his corpse. His suit and gear were obtained."

"That about wraps everything up. Hopefully, Benjamin was able to get a copy of the list of scientific rivals so we can investigate the rumors around the world more efficiently. A job well done as always, all things considered."

"Not everything has been accounted for, sir." Abraham gulped again, and his whole body shook for a second. "The servants became detached from our company, sir. I think they fell in love with the life they were living."

"Impossible. I raised those two as if they were my own flesh and blood, their genes almost as if they were my own! Their hearts were hardened, their minds set, and their eyes and ears active. Why would they betray us? Benjamin failed to do his job properly, and before you even tell me, I already know about Elizabeth's pregnancy."

"I believe it's because of the similarity between you and Kronos, sir! Benjamin grew as fond of Kronos as he was of you. More importantly, women tend to fall in love with men like their fathers. In fact, I've heard about this one man who said that daughters would marry their fathers and love them if not turned away from such a thing due to society. It's the only reason why Elizabeth fell in love with Kronos and his empire. She confused it with her love for you and this company."

"I know the man of whom you speak, Abraham, as I have been around for a long time and know all things. While your point is a valid one, I'm afraid it's not just that. Kronos also made her love him on purpose as a slap across the face to our company. Not only has he preserved his genius by creating an offspring who will be just as intelligent as him if not more, but he also did it with one of our own agents. He knew she was a spy, and now he's used her to threaten us, mock us, damage our pride, and to piss me off. He's one smart son of a bitch."

"What are we to do about Elizabeth and the child? She's currently on the run, but we should be able to capture her. He'd technically be your grandchild. The blasphemous birth of that unholy child could lead to another Kronos existing, which jeopardizes all of our work."

"Yes, but this time... I'm going to raise him myself," Gene replied as a sinister grin lit up his face and he chuckled menacingly to himself.

Abraham gulped. "Understood. I'll try my best to capture the pregnant woman and prevent her from killing the child."

"Excellent."

"Oh, and there's one last thing... G.O.D."

"I can tell that this is *really* going to piss me off. I spent a long time in Texas. You don't want to make me angry."

"I'm afraid so, sir. Unfortunately, and I don't even know how, but one of the scientists survived. Besides the possibility of Damon's survival, that is."

Gene looked at Abraham with a petrifying gaze. "Are you sure?"

"Yes, sir," Abraham said with a gulp, terrified. His whole face dripping with sweat, his entire body trembled, including his fake leg. "One of your seven creations is still alive, and we have reason to believe that they're coming for us with everything they've got."

www.ingramcontent.com/pod-product-compliance
Lightning Source LLC
Chambersburg PA
CBHW051655060726
47593CB00022B/2046